KATHERINE

More Than Friends

A Saving Grace Novel

HARCOURT, INC.

Orlando   Austin   New York   San Diego   London

www.HarcourtBooks.com

Library of Congress Cataloging-in-Publication Data
Spencer, Katherine.
More than friends: a Saving Grace novel/Katherine Spencer.
p.   cm.
Summary: When the mysterious Philomena suggests that Grace Stanley get a job where her deceased brother's best friend, Jackson, works, the romance that quickly develops becomes complicated when Grace realizes that Jackson is stealing from the store.
[1. Stealing—Fiction.   2. Conduct of life—Fiction.
3. Stores, Retail—Fiction.   4. Dating (Social customs)—Fiction.
5. Spiritual life—Fiction.]   I. Title.
PZ7.S74813Mor   2008
[Fic]—dc22   2007030196
ISBN 978-0-15-205746-6

Text set in Perpetua
Designed by Linda Lockowitz

First edition
H G F E D C B A

Printed in the United States of America

One

I STOOD ON THE SIDEWALK, gazing at the shop window. ALTERNATE REALITIES—A WHOLE EARTH EMPORIUM, the sign painted on it said. The pale green letters curled like leafy vines. I had never been able to decide if the effect was New Age retro or just plain outdated. It didn't matter, though. I had loved Alternate Realities since the day my brother, Matt, and I first discovered it.

Since then, I had spent hours looking at the exotic objects they stocked from every part of the globe, while Matt nearly inhaled their music department, buying CDs, guitar strings, and once, a mandolin that he never played, not ever. Realities, as the locals call it, has stuff for everyone, and the whole place is really cool. My friends and I consider it about the only truly interesting store in Greenwood, Ohio.

Philomena Cantos stood beside me, peering at the window display of hand-painted tables and chairs from Mexico. "This is it," she said. "This is where you should apply for a job."

"Have you even been in there?" I asked, surprised.

Philomena and I have been friends for the last few months, but I'd never seen her go into a place like Alternate Realities. Come to think of it, I'd never seen her shop for anything.

"No. I don't go into stores much," she said.

Philomena may be the only sixteen-year-old girl in all of Ohio who would make a statement like that. But Philomena is not exactly like other people. In fact, she's weird. I know this sounds crazy—but I'm pretty sure there's something otherworldly about Philomena. Wait . . . that sounds like she's an alien. She's different but she's not *that* different. . . . It's just that she told me she was sent to help me, and I'm pretty sure she meant God sent her—which is really strange, because ever since my brother, Matt died, God and I haven't been on such good terms.

But there I was last Friday, sipping my mocha latte when Philomena suddenly appeared at my side. (She has a habit of mysteriously doing that.)

"What are you doing next Tuesday after school?" she asked.

Before I could answer, Phil suggested we meet and go job hunting. Job hunting for me, that is.

I hadn't planned on getting a job. But I made some not-so-outstanding choices a few months ago,

2

at the beginning of my junior year. This past summer, Matt was killed in a car crash that I still more than half believe was my fault. Not that I caused the accident. I wasn't even there. Matt went out to run an errand I should have taken care of . . . and never came back.

His death left me pretty messed up. I started doing things I shouldn't have. Stupid, hazardous-to-one's-health things like drinking. And I racked up some serious credit-card debt. I used the card that was supposed to be "just for emergencies" on hot clothes to go with the new "cool" friends I was hanging with.

When my parents discovered what I had done, they made it clear that I was responsible for paying them back. Which meant I needed a job and I needed it now.

So there we were, spending Tuesday afternoon after school pounding the pavement along Main Street, Greenwood's old downtown. It used to be rundown and sort of seedy. But in the last few years, it's been undergoing what my English teacher, Ms. Kaplanski, would probably call a *renaissance,* a rebirth. There are a bunch of cool, funky shops on Main Street now. Restaurants and coffee bars with Wifi. No chain stores, like at the mall.

Alternate Realities is one of the biggest, and oldest, businesses on Main Street. It started out as a five-and-dime, complete with lunch counter. A couple of years ago, the building was almost condemned. Then, Ms. Newberry came to town and turned it into a sort of cosmic general store. Now there are departments for clothes, books, music, household goods, even furniture, most of it imported and exotic.

In her slightly baggy leggings and oversized tunic sweater, I have to admit Philomena looked like she belonged here. As if drawn by a homing beacon, she began to make her way toward the food section in the far corner.

"I hear they make great smoothies."

"From who?" I asked. The thing is, I almost never see Philomena talking to other kids. She transferred to our school at the beginning of the year and—I have to say it—she's about as geeky as they come. I wasn't even sure I liked her at first. I don't think her lack of a social life bothers her much. Philomena has other priorities.

"Oh, I just hear things," she said, sending me a look over her shoulder. I can never quite decide what color her eyes are. It's just one of the slightly unnerving things about her.

"No doubt," I muttered.

"I hear you can have them make any combination you want," she continued as we began to weave our way past shelves lined with rows of brightly colored dishes. "I'm thinking of mango/raspberry/banana/kiwi. What do you think?"

I opened my mouth to give the only truthful answer I could: *gross.* But before it came out, we heard a terrific crash up ahead and to the right. A shower of broken pottery shot into the aisle.

"Oh, *dear,*" said an exasperated voice.

Philomena started to run, skidding to a stop as she reached the intersection.

"Is there anything we can do to help?" she asked.

I got there just as a woman in a long dress with what I swore was the same sort of leafy design pattern as the writing on the shop window turned around. Long, curly, red hair tumbled over her shoulders. Her feet were thrust into a pair of Birkenstocks.

Ms. Newberry, the shop's owner, aka earth mother. It was a look that actually seemed to suit her, I have to admit.

She put her hands on her hips and gazed at Philomena through slightly widened eyes. "I don't suppose you're looking for a job."

Philomena smiled. "I already have one," she admitted. Then, quick as lightning, she reached out and put her hand on my arm. "But my friend, Grace, needs one. Maybe you would consider her?"

Ms. Newberry tilted her head, and I found myself the focus of her dark brown eyes. She regarded me steadily for a moment, and I was suddenly aware of Philomena's hand on my arm, sending me a great big positive vibe.

5

"Grace," Ms. Newberry suddenly said, pronouncing my name as if this would cement it in her mind.

"Grace Stanley," I filled in.

Ms. Newberry gave a brisk nod. "All right, then, Grace Stanley," she said. "Let's get you suited up. A blue apron, I think. Deep blue for serenity and clarity. Always a fine way to start something new, don't you agree?"

Without waiting for an answer, she turned on one heel, stepped around the pile of broken dishes, and set off down the aisle.

Philomena gave my arm an excited squeeze. "See?" she whispered. "I knew we should come in here."

I couldn't quite believe what had just happened. Ms. Newberry didn't even ask me for references or to fill out an application.

Ms. Newberry turned back around, her expression surprised. "Well, is there some reason you can't start right away?"

I felt Philomena's hand drop away. I took a breath, and told the truth.

"Not a single, solitary one," I answered with a smile.

Several tasks later and a phone call to my parents to give them the good news, I was finally ready to head for home. My head was a blur of Alternate Realities info. I guess you could say I had entered an alternate reality of my own.

After sweeping up the broken dishes, my first duty as a new AR employee had been to learn to operate the smoothie maker, so I could make Philomena whatever kind she wanted, free of charge. This was Ms. Newberry's way of thanking her for bringing me in.

Phil had departed, happily slurping her mango/raspberry/banana/kiwi/flaxseed wonder. I could catch up with her at school the next day, assuming she survived the drink.

The rest of my first shift had included a store tour and an introduction to the stockroom, where everything but the food items were stored. If I remembered even half of it, it would be a miracle.

I was coming out of the storeroom with one last armload of dishes when I ran into about the last person I expected to see: Jackson Turner.

"Grace," he said, his voice sounding just as surprised as I felt. I watched as his eyes took in the fact that I was wearing a store apron. "When did you start working here? Hi."

Jackson was a year ahead of me at school. He and Matt had been best friends. They were always playing music together and had formed a band, the Daily Dose. I even had a crush on Jackson at one point. Typical, I guess. Don't younger sisters always end up crushing on their older brother's best friends?

Still, there was something special about Jackson. His hair was a sort of dirty blond, always slightly messy, in a rock star sort of way. Now, though, his hair was brushed and he was wearing a bright red Alternate Realities T-shirt.

"About two hours ago," I answered. "Hi, yourself."

Jackson had been in the car when Matt ran that errand for me. Jackson had emerged without a scrape while Matt had lost his life.

For a long time, I hated Jackson for it. Why should he still be here when Matt wasn't? Bit by bit, though, I'd gotten over feeling that way, something else I had to give Philomena credit for. She helped me see that you can't blame a person for surviving, any more than you can blame the one who died.

Still, Matt's death made things complicated between Jackson and me.

Jackson smiled. "That apron looks good on you," he said. "Blue for serenity and clarity, I see."

"I like the T-shirt better," I admitted.

"It just depends on what your regular department is, he explained. "Music, clothing, and I think furniture get to wear T-shirts."

"What's your color mean?"

8

I thought I saw a shadow cross Jackson's face as he answered, "Optimism."

"It could be hokier," I said. "I mean, it could be red for . . . enthusiasm."

He gave me a half smile, but I was definitely seeing a shadow now. Not just in Jackson's face but also in his eyes. I shifted the pile of plates in my arms. All of a sudden, they were feeling pretty heavy.

"Let me help you with those," Jackson said. "I just got off shift, so Ms. Newberry won't mind."

He took the stack of plates from me, and we walked across the glossy hardwood floor toward the housewares section. Or HOME EMBELLISHMENTS, as the sign above the department declared.

"Don't tell me," I said, trying to lighten the mood a bit. "You work in the music department, right?"

Jackson nodded. "Got it in one. It's pretty cool. Dave Harper, the guy who manages the section, is actually starting to let me handle the department on my own sometimes."

"Cool," I said.

We reached the embellishments department. I did a quick restock of the shelf, then stood back to make sure I had arranged things the way Ms. Newberry wanted.

"I gotta hand it to you, Grace," Jackson commented. "Nobody stacks plates the way you do."

"Ha ha," I said. "Very funny." I pulled in a breath.

"So," I said, as nonchalantly as I could. "Now that the plates are perfectly stacked, I'm outta here. Are you heading home?"

Jackson only lived a couple of blocks from my house. He and Matt always used to walk home from school together.

"Uh-huh." He nodded. His eyes glanced into mine, then looked away. "We could walk together, if you like."

"That sounds great," I said. "Let me just ditch this apron, okay?"

"Sure," Jackson said. "I'll meet you out front."

"So, how long have you been working at Realities?" I asked a few minutes later.

"About three months, since the end of summer."

Right after Matt died, I thought.

"The band is trying to put together a CD. Not just a demo, a real, professional one. We're all paying a share. My folks won't give me any money for it, so here I am."

"I thought they supported your music," I said, surprised.

He was quiet for a moment, a frown snaking down between his eyebrows. "My parents are splitting up," he finally said.

I don't know what I'd expected him to say,

but that sure wasn't it. No wonder Ms. Newberry thought he needed a little optimism.

Not only did the Turners live in our neighborhood, they went to the same church we did. I didn't know Jackson's parents well, but they had always seemed nice. I never saw them argue or anything. Jackson has a little brother, Sam, who was eleven. I wondered how he felt about the divorce.

"Wow," I said, then winced at how incredibly lame I sounded. "That's tough. When did all this happen?"

Jackson gave a shrug. If he was hoping to show he didn't care, he failed pretty miserably. He had sort of a pinched look around his mouth, and his shoulders slumped.

"They've been fighting for a while. Like . . . since before I was born." He shook his head, as if to dispel some ugly inner vision. "I got kind of used to it. I could tune it out most of the time. Then one day, everything collapsed. I'm still not sure what set things off.

"When Sam and I came home from school, my parents were yelling so loud we could hear them out on the sidewalk. My dad moved out that night. He's living in Chicago now. Mom is totally frantic. She worries about money all the time. Sometimes I think she's more worried about that than about Sam or me."

"That totally sucks," I said. I thought about my

parents and how horrible it would be if they suddenly split.

"So tell me about the CD," I said, deliberately changing the subject. "How long do you think it will take to put it together?"

"That's the million-dollar question. Not that it will cost that much," he joked. Talking about music seemed to make Jackson feel better. "Depends on how hard we work and how fast we can scrape together the money," he went on. "We're picking out the tunes we want to record now. Then we'll have to find a studio and rent time."

"Just like you and Matt always talked about," I said, without thinking, then bit down, hard, on the tip of my tongue.

Losing Matt hadn't just left a gaping hole in my life. It left one in Jackson's, too. I knew Jackson missed him nearly as much as I did. After the accident, Jackson and I talked about Matt only a few times. It was just too hard.

This time, Jackson surprised me. "We're going to record a lot of Matt's music," he said. "I really want Matt's songs to get out there, to have other people hear them."

The band had played Matt's music at a concert a few months ago. It had been hard for me to go, at first, but when I heard them I knew Matt would have loved it. The concert turned out to be a really good thing—for me and Jackson and the band, even for my folks.

"So," he went on. "I was wondering. You know there's this big Battle of the Bands thing coming up?"

Battle of the Bands was a competition that the town hosted every year. Alternate Realities was even one of the sponsors. Bands from all over the area come to play in this sort of round-robin competition. If a band is lucky, they'll get picked up by a promoter.

"We're going to do a sort of demo CD—the best of the Daily Dose—to sell at the Battle," Jackson went on. "All the bands do it. Lots of them look pretty cut-rate. But you're a really good artist, and I was thinking—if we had some really great artwork for the cover . . ."

"Sure. I'd love to do something for you guys," I said. I liked the idea of being included in something that Matt was once part of. "Do you have something special in mind?"

"Just something cool," Jackson said, with a shrug. "Otherwise, we'll end up with something totally lame. Charlie wants to go to an auto show and take pictures of vintage cars."

I laughed. That was a lame idea, and it sounded just like Charlie. He's the band's drummer.

"I think I can do better than that," I said. "For

instance, something that actually relates to the band might be nice."

This time, it was Jackson who laughed. As he did, he turned his head and looked straight into my eyes.

Oh, wow, I thought.

It was a movie moment for sure. One of those moments that's completely unexpected but that changes everything. That means something. In this case, I was pretty sure I knew what it meant: I wasn't alone when it came to crushing. And my crush hadn't gone away. Not by a long shot.

Then, quickly as it had come on, the moment was over. A car honked its horn. Jackson and I both jumped at the exact same time.

"Hey, this is my street," Jackson said as if he hadn't realized we'd come so far.

I felt a pang of disappointment. He would turn off now. There wasn't really any reason for him to walk me all the way home.

"So, I guess I'll see you around," I said, feeling awkward all of a sudden. Had something just happened between us or hadn't it? If the answer was *yes,* what was I going to do about it?

"It was great to see you," I went on. "Since we're both working at Realities, I guess it'll—you know—happen more often."

For crying out loud, Grace, I thought. *Could you sound more like a total dork?*

"Yeah. I guess it will," Jackson said. For just a split second, I thought he was going to say something more. Instead, he turned to go.

"Jackson," I called. "I'm really sorry about what's happening with your family. I know it must be tough . . ." Jackson turned back as my voice trailed off. "Thanks," he said quietly. He didn't seem angry about the situation, the way he had been earlier. Now he just seemed tired. "Just think about that CD cover, okay?"

"Okay," I said.

But it wasn't the CD cover I thought about all the way home. Instead, it was the way I had felt when Jackson's eyes gazed down into mine.

When I got home that night my mother was in the kitchen, making dinner. She still had on her work clothes: a silk blouse, a navy blue skirt, and gold earrings. She'd lost the high heels and matching blazer. These were her "super salesperson" real-estate-lady clothes. She didn't always get that dressed up for work, so I guessed she must have had an open house or a big meeting with a client.

Our dog, Wiley, was lying under the table, his head on his paws but big eyes watchful, waiting for something edible to fall his way. His long tail thumped on the floor when I walked into the room.

"Hi, Grace," my mom said. "Congratulations on the job. How are things so far?"

"Okay," I replied. I sat down at the table and stroked Wiley's head. He scrambled up to sit next to me, leaning against my leg with doggy devotion. "A lot of new things to learn, but I think I'll be okay. Ms. Newberry seems pretty nice."

Mom glanced at me sympathetically. "First days at a new job are always hard. My guess is you'll be happy there in no time."

I debated with myself about mentioning that Jackson worked at AR, then decided against it. I think my mom has felt awkward around him since the accident. Instead, I gave Wiley's head a last scratch, got up, walked into the pantry, and snagged a box of crackers to tide me over till whatever Mom was making was ready.

"What's for dinner?" I asked.

"Roast chicken and stir-fried vegetables," my mother replied. "I've got bok choy, straw mushrooms, and bean sprouts. Look to see if we've still got a can of bamboo shoots, will you?"

"Sure." I put the crackers away, grabbed the can of bamboo shoots, and set them on the counter beside her. "You should really put an apron on," I said. "You don't want to splatter oil all over your best power suit. Ms. Newberry had me wear a deep blue apron today, for serenity and clarity."

My mother chuckled, but she went and got her apron. "Want to set the table? Your father should be home any minute."

I nodded. *Looks like dishes are going to be my specialty,* I thought. I began to set the table, my mom and I working in companionable silence while we waited for my dad to come home.

As soon as we finished dinner, it would be homework time. I only had a small ton. Having an after-school job was definitely going to cut into my downtime. No more long sessions of IMing my friends or experimenting in front of the bathroom mirror with new hairdos and makeup. Not that my experiments had ever produced any spectacular results.

I wasn't sure how I felt about giving up my free time. But I *was* sure I didn't have a choice. Some mistakes you make you just have to pay for. Literally.

I heard the front door slam and the scramble of Wiley's paws on the kitchen floor as he took off to greet my father.

"Something smells good," Dad announced as he came through the kitchen door. He gave my mom a quick kiss, then tousled my hair the way he used to do when I was small.

"Grace got a job," my mom announced, then clapped a hand across her mouth. "I should have let you tell. I'm sorry, honey."

"That's great," my dad said. He washed his hands at the kitchen sink, then sat at the table. All business, as usual. "Where and when do you start?"

"Alternate Realities," I answered, as I brought the stir-fried veggies over to the table. "And I already started. Ms. Newberry, the owner, hired me and put me to work this afternoon."

"That's great, Grace," my dad said, as my mom set the roast chicken on the table. "That's a really good first step."

I sighed. That was typical of my dad's compliments. Why couldn't he have just said *that's great* and be done with it?

I sat down in my chair, and Wiley crawled under the table and put his head on my feet.

"How many hours will you be working?" my mom asked.

"We're still sorting that out," I replied. "But we're talking about three afternoons during the week and sometimes on Saturdays."

"Sounds reasonable," my father said. He helped himself to chicken and vegetables, then passed them to me. "Let's see how it goes." He shot my mother a quick look across the table.

Here is comes, I thought. *The lecture.*

"Just remember that you can't afford to let the job affect your schoolwork, honey," he went on. "This is an important year. You need to keep your grades up."

"I know that, Dad," I said.

Boy, did I ever. My dad has always had this obsession with college and getting into a "good" school, even before I screwed up. He's so obsessed, Matt and I actually made up a secret game about it.

Matt claimed that any concept in the English language could remind my father of college. So I would say something like "dill pickle" and Matt would imitate my dad, using whatever I suggested in a sentence that related to college.

"I hear they serve wonderful dill pickles in the dorms at Yale. You could go to Yale, you know. If you keep your grades up."

I nearly looked over to the empty place where my brother used to sit, about to share a secret look. I caught myself just in time.

"If you're not working this Saturday," my mother said, "maybe you'd like to help out at the church coat drive."

"I'm not sure I can," I replied. "I promised my friends I'd go with them to Fall Fair at school. That's for a good cause, too. The school clubs."

My mother was silent for a moment. I could see that she wasn't happy with my answer. "They'll be collecting for a few more weeks. Maybe you can come another time."

The youth group at our church runs a collection every fall, and we give out coats to people in need.

I usually help out. But ever since Matt died, spending time at church for any reason makes me uncomfortable. I've gotten a little better that way, but I was hardly back to being a regular. Unlike my parents, who seemed to find comfort in our church and in talking to our minister, Pastor James.

"Okay," I said. "Just keep me posted. Would it be okay if I just headed straight upstairs now? I've got a massive amount of homework."

"I think your father can handle the dishes for once," my mother said. My father gave a grunt, but didn't object.

"Thanks, Mom," I said, getting up from the table. "I'll come down in a little while and grab some dessert."

As I headed up the stairs to my room, I could hear my father's voice and my mother's low reply. Talking about me, no doubt. I made it to my room, and quietly closed the door behind me.

I was going to do homework. I definitely was. Just as soon as I checked who was online. To sort of clear my head and get me in the mood. I switched on my computer and went straight to my buddy list.

Two of my best friends, Andy and Rebecca, were on. I told them about the job, but we didn't get much further before they both had to sign off.

I was just about to sign off myself, when someone new messaged me. JackFlash88—*That's Jackson!* I thought.

```
JackFlash88: Hey, Grace. U make it
             home all right?

GraceS_Full: Those last few blocks
             always kind of tricky.
             I managed 2 survive.

JackFlash88: Outstanding. Been
             thinking abt the CD
             cover. Really hope
             you'll give it a shot.
```

That sounded promising.

```
GraceS_Full: Let me go through some
             of my art tonight. Will
             bring stuff to school
             tomorrow. Just 4 ideas. OK?

JackFlash88: Sounds great. U working
             tomorrow? I'm off. Band
             practice at my house.
             4:30. U could bring art
             here and show everyone.
```

Jackson was inviting me over to his house?

I was glad the conversation was online so he couldn't see the way I was blushing.

```
GraceS_Full: Can do. Thanks 4 the
             invite.

JackFlash88: Great. Remember where I
             live?
```

As if I was likely to forget.

```
GraceS_Full: I think so. See U
             tomorrow.
```

We both signed off and I turned on my away message, but instead of starting my homework, I pulled out a bunch of artwork I kept in a portfolio under my bed.

I took out some pieces I had done in the last year, the ones I was saving for my college applications. Though my dad might never approve, I was planning to study art in college.

I flipped through a bunch of sketches and figure drawings, a few decent wood-block prints, and a collage with computer graphics. Not to mention a whole lot of what I think of as stream-of-consciousness stuff. Quick sketches of anything and everything that caught my eye—dogs, trees, an old hat. I should have asked Jackson if the band had a title for the CD.

I spread everything out on the floor and looked it over. *What would Matt have chosen?* I wondered. He would have had plenty of outrageous ideas, I knew that much. I didn't even have to close my eyes to imagine him pawing through my portfolio, finding ones he liked and tossing ideas around left and right.

"Don't stop here, Grace," he would have said. "The sky's the limit. Don't hold back."

Oh, Matt, I thought. *I miss you so much.*

I had tried so hard to make the pain go away. I'd made it recede, but it was never really gone. But maybe working on the CD cover would make me feel more connected to Matt again, would somehow ease the pain.

The phone rang then and I picked it up.

"Hi, Grace." It was Philomena, and somehow I knew it was no accident that she called just when I was missing Matt so much.

From the day I first met her, nothing about our friendship had been normal. Philomena was the one who pulled me back into the land of the living when I fell into my self-destruct mode right after Matt died. She wouldn't give up on me and she got me through it. Then she told me she had been sent to help me. And I believed her.

"How was the first day on the job?" she asked.

"It went fine," I said warily. "Philomena, how come you led me right to Alternate Realities? Did you know I haven't been there for ages? Did you know Ms. Newberry was going to offer me a job?"

Philomena sighed. "No. I'm not a fortune-teller. I just had a . . . feeling. That you would like it there."

"Oh, sure. A feeling," I said, not trying to disguise my skepticism.

"Do you remember when we talked about working together?"

"Sure," I said, "but don't tell me you're planning to get a job at Realities, are you?"

"Just the opposite," she said. "I think Realities is a place that needs *your* help."

Maybe I was finally beginning to break the Philomena code. "You took me there because you want me to help Ms. Newberry, right? Sort of the way you helped me?"

Philomena was silent. Maybe I hadn't broken the code.

"It may not be at the store," she said at last. "Just watch and you'll be able to tell when you're needed."

"Oh, that clears up everything," I muttered.

Philomena laughed. "See you in school tomorrow," she said. "And, Grace—I'm glad we're going to be working together."

Two

BY THE NEXT MORNING, it was clear I was going to have to make some radical changes in my lifestyle. Or maybe I should say, the job was going to require me to make some radical changes. Ones I wasn't all that sure I was going to like.

To start things off, I had been up until one, slaving on my homework without even getting close to being done. To compensate, I set my alarm for six A.M., thinking I would get up early and work some more.

Right, Grace. Dream on.

Which is exactly what happened when the alarm rang.

I slept through that early buzzer, then my usual one, too. My mother had to drive me to school, and I missed hanging out with my friends before first period. I didn't get to tell them about seeing Jackson.

Not quite the start to the day I had in mind.

At lunchtime, I headed straight to the cafeteria, looking for my friends. Fifth-period lunch is the most crowded but the best for people watching.

I spotted my group at our usual table, third one down on the left side, near the courtyard windows. It's funny, but it's almost like we have assigned seating in the cafeteria. Once a group stakes out a spot, that's their territory and everybody pretty much respects the claim.

Everyone except Dana Sloan and her crowd, our school's idea of ultimate cool. They make a point of sitting anywhere they please, usually wherever they'll get the most attention. Dana and her friends have the best hair, the most expensive clothes, the coolest shoes, and the whitest teeth. They were always going skiing in Utah or spending Christmas in Antigua. Their tans look exactly the same all year round. Not too long ago, back in September when I wanted to change my whole life, I hung with them. Talk about mistakes . . .

"Hey, Grace. What's up?" I heard Dana's voice.

"Not much," I answered, forcing myself to slow down. I wished she hadn't noticed me, wished I were already at my own table, sitting with my friends.

But I knew the rule: Never let predators see you sweat.

"How about you?" I asked. "What's up?"

"Oh," Dana waved a hand in the air, as if she were drying a fresh coat of nail polish. "Not too much. Did you do your DBQs?"

DBQs! I thought with a surge of panic. I knew there was something I had forgotten. And American History was next period.

DBQs stands for document-based questions. First you read the text of an actual old document, say a speech made in some long-ago Congress. Then, you answer questions about it. Sometimes Ms. Hudson, the history teacher, collects them and sometimes she doesn't. The catch is, you never know when she's going to do what. It's sort of like a homework assignment and a pop quiz all rolled into one.

"I didn't finish," I admitted. "Did you?"

Dana nodded, giving me a smug smile. I would bet my first paycheck she paid her housekeeper to do it for her. Dana paid her to type her papers all the time.

"So, Grace," Lindsay Wexler put in, staring at me from under a veil of dark shiny hair, an expression I couldn't quite read in her cat-green eyes. "Didn't I see you yesterday at Alternate Realities, wearing one of those dorky aprons? What gives? Do you have a job there or something?"

"I do," I said. "I just started yesterday."

Lindsay made a face. "That place is so weird."

"I wouldn't mind getting a job in a really good clothing store or something," Dana put in. "You can get a huge discount when you buy stuff."

"I'd just rather go shopping, like a normal person," Lindsay said.

I almost laughed. Lindsay's idea of "shopping, like a normal person" was dropping $150 on a T-shirt and $400 on designer jeans. Lindsay was the one who had egged me on when I shopped myself into credit-card debt. Not that it was her fault. I was the one who whipped out the card.

"I kind of like Alternate Realities," Morgan offered, taking a dainty sip of her diet soda. "They sell these great low-carb energy bars."

I have never met anyone as utterly obsessed by food as Morgan.

"Please," Lindsay said with a roll of her eyes. "Those things taste like chalk. Give me chocolate any day." She got up, yanked down the back of her black miniskirt and smoothed out the front of her v-neck wrap top.

"I need to get some chem notes. Good luck with your job, Grace."

She strolled over to a table of senior guys, flashing a megawatt smile. Her departure seemed to be the signal that I was free to go.

I reached my friends' table, dropped my backpack onto the tabletop, and sank down onto the bench.

"Whew!" I said.

"I thought you were on the lunch menu there for a moment," my friend Andy Chin remarked.

Andy's the true-blue type. Quiet and incredibly smart. I knew she would think my job was cool. Alternate Realities is an Andy kind of store. She's a vegetarian, and even has a sticker on her backpack that proclaims: MEAT IS MURDER. Now, her comment made me laugh out loud. The thing most people don't realize about Andy because she's so quiet is that she's also very funny.

"So did I," I admitted. "Guess I'm just not as tasty as I used to be."

Rebecca Giomi rolled her eyes. "It's amazing you can even hold a civil conversation with them."

I've known Rebecca the longest of all my friends, since second grade. She's solid, totally reliable.

Sara Kramer, the fourth and final member of our group, and our resident drama queen, leaned forward, as if about to confide a really juicy secret.

"Before we were so rudely interrupted online last night—my parents, the Neanderthals, decided that I spend too much time on the computer—you said you were working at Alternate Realities. So tell us." Sara took on the tone of TV talk show host. "We want to hear every single thing about it."

"There's not all that much to tell," I said. "I've only worked there for a couple of hours."

I paused, and three pairs of eyes gazed at me expectantly.

"There is one unexpected job benefit, though. And I don't mean free smoothies."

Sara gave a little wriggle of excitement. "I knew it. Didn't I say I knew it? Spill everything, Grace Stanley, right this second. We're your best friends. It's what we live for."

"I think you mean it's what we're *here* for, Sara," Andy said.

Sara gave a completely unembarrassed laugh. "No, I don't!"

"Jackson Turner works in the music department," I said. "We got off shift at the same time, and he pretty much walked me home."

"Okay," Rebecca said. "That news is definitely hot."

"Well, but wait a minute," Sara said, "I thought you didn't like Jackson anymore."

"For crying out loud, Sara. Just look at her," Andy said. "Of course she likes him. She's redder than an organic tomato at just one mention of his name."

"I am not!" I said. I touched my hands to my cheeks. "Am I? And it's not like that . . . not exactly."

"Then what is it like?" Andy inquired.

"His band wants to make a CD that includes some of Matt's music," I said. "Jackson asked if I would do some artwork for the cover." I took a breath then told them the rest. "He IM'd me last night and asked me to come over to his house this afternoon."

Sara's eyes widened. "Rebecca's right," she announced. "That news *is* definitely hot. Are you going?"

"Of course she's going." Andy turned to me. "You're going, right?"

"Absolutely," I nodded. "The band is coming over for a practice. Jackson wants me to show everybody my artwork."

"But you'll get some one-on-one time, right?" Rebecca asked.

"I have no idea," I answered. "I think so."

I hope so, I thought.

"You will, Grace," Andy said supportively. "Jackson likes you. I've always thought so."

"Me, too." Rebecca nodded vigorously.

"He is pretty cute. I love his hair." Sara sighed. "I can't wait to hear what happens next. This is all just so exciting."

"I'm just taking over some artwork for a CD cover, Sara," I said with a laugh.

"Oh, no. It's much more than that," she countered. "And we all expect a full report."

"Absolutely. Or no math help," Andy remarked. Andy was the one getting me through trig.

"I'll send you all an e-mail, as soon as I get home," I promised.

All of a sudden, Rebecca's expression changed. Her eyes narrowed and she got a funny little crease straight across the middle of her forehead that she only gets when she's really upset.

"What is it, Rebecca?" I asked. "What's wrong?"

"Lindsay Wexler," she said succinctly.

I turned to follow Rebecca's gaze and saw Lindsay, still hanging out at the table of senior dudes. She was sitting on the table now, swinging her long legs. You could practically watch all the guys' heads move every time her legs did.

"Can you believe that?" Rebecca asked in a tight voice. I'm pretty sure she was clenching her jaw. The only other times I'd seen her look this fierce were on the lacrosse field during play-off games.

Andy glanced over as well. "What's not to believe? She's just doing the same thing she does every day: hitting on some guy."

"I think you mean *guys*," Sara said. "She's already gone through practically every guy in the senior class. Who's left?"

"Scott Hammond," Rebecca ground out. "He's just nice enough not to see her for what she really is. With my luck, he'll fall for her."

I hadn't noticed Scott Hammond as part of Lindsay's captive audience, but I did now. And a little bell went off.

"You mean the guy in your chem lab? Scott-Drop-and-Roll?"

Rebecca shot an unamused glance in my direction. *Something is definitely up here,* I thought. Every other time I had mentioned the stupid nickname I made up for him, she had at least smiled.

Scott Hammond was a senior; tall, dark, and pretty cute. Into sports, but not a brainless, jerky jock. He was in Rebecca's chem lab, and she'd had a major crush on him since the first day of school.

She had been petrified to talk to him, though. The truth is, Rebecca is pretty shy. Scott might never have noticed her if she hadn't accidentally tipped over her Bunsen burner and nearly set the entire school on fire. Quick-thinking Scott had smothered the mess with a sweatshirt. Ever since then, I called him Scott-Drop-and-Roll. From the annual fire-prevention assembly, in elementary school.

Maybe you had to be there to get the joke.

"I wouldn't worry too much about it, Becca," I said now. "Like Sara said, Lindsay goes after a lot of guys. She could be after Scott today and some other guy tomorrow."

"There, you see?" Sara spoke up supportively. "Besides, Scott may be nice, but he isn't stupid."

Just at that moment, Lindsay boosted herself down from the table and strolled back to Dana and Morgan, looking altogether too pleased with herself.

The pack of guys she had been flirting with got up and left, including Scott Hammond. Rebecca sat back and opened a notebook. I could tell she didn't want to talk about this anymore. I was pretty sure she thought Lindsay had somehow just won Scott.

But things aren't always what they appear to be. At least that's what Philomena told me.

As if my thoughts had summoned her, Philomena suddenly came into view, walking toward our table, a stack of books in the crook of her arm. My other friends knew Philomena, but she wasn't quite part of our group. We didn't exactly all hang out together.

"Hi, Grace. Hi, everybody." Phil sounded cheerful as ever.

Everyone said hello, but I noticed Andy and Sara exchange a quick look. Rebecca continued to stare down at her notebook.

Philomena was wearing another of her "what not to wear" . . . *ever* specials. I have no idea where she gets her ideas about clothes. Today she had on a pale yellow button-down shirt with navy blue corduroy pants. Not hip huggers or jeans, but the kind of pants moms wear, with pleats in the front and a waistline up to her chin. Her long, dark hair was pushed back and held in place with a wide hair band. I hadn't even seen one of those since about second grade.

Okay, I needed help with my life, but Philomena needed lots of help with her fashion. Come to think of it, maybe I could help Philomena turn into a fashionista. I laughed at the thought.

"So, did you tell everyone about your new job at Alternate Realities?" she asked brightly. Her gaze took in the rest of my friends. "Isn't it great that Grace is working there? I knew she would love it."

"How did you know?" Rebecca asked, looking up.

"What?"

"You said Grace would love working at Alternate Realities," Rebecca echoed Philomena's words back to her. "How did you know it?"

Philomena's eyes widened and she looked directly at Rebecca. "I guess it was just instinct," she finally answered. "There's such a good feeling there that I knew Grace would be drawn in and feel welcome."

"Well, I am glad I took the job," I said, before Rebecca could continue her interrogation. I gathered up my trash and made a neat ball for the bin. "I forgot about my DBQs for history, and I didn't finish the reading assignment for English, either. I'd better hide out someplace and get some work done."

I got up, hoping Phil would get the hint and tag along. The dynamic between her and my other friends was definitely starting to weird me out.

This was something I was going to have to deal

with, I realized. How was I going to explain about Phil—especially if I started spending more time with her?

"Hey, Philomena," Sara suddenly spoke up. "Are you volunteering at the school fair on Saturday? I thought I saw your name on the sign-up sheet."

"Yes. I'm working for the yearbook," Philomena said with an enthusiastic nod. Her head band slipped back a little on her head. Maybe if we were all lucky, it would fall off and she would never notice it was gone.

"I'm still not clear about how it all works, though. Does every club have their own booth?"

"Yeah, you haven't seen the chart that shows where everyone is going to be?" Sara got to her feet and picked up her empty tray. "This year they hid it in the AV room. Come on, I'll show you."

Philomena walked off with Sara. Andy announced she was heading to the library. Rebecca and I were left alone.

"Want me to bring you up to speed on the English assignment?" Rebecca asked.

"Sure," I said. Becca pulled out her copy of *The Great Gatsby* and flipped to a page marked with a yellow Post-it.

"Becca," I said. "Are you all right? You seem . . . I don't know."

"I don't know, either," she said with a sudden laugh. "I think that's part of the problem." She ran her finger back and forth across the edge of the Post-it note.

"Grace," she said. "Don't you think Philomena is just a bit—I don't know—odd? Not that she isn't nice," she went on quickly. "It's just . . . she's so strange."

"She—"

"Let me finish. When you got all caught up with Dana Sloan and her crew, I didn't like it but I understood. Anyone would have a hard time resisting a personal invite to hang out at Dana's. But I guess I just don't understand what Philomena's big appeal is. I mean, what do we really know about her?"

What did I *really* know? Next to nothing. What I thought I knew, though, now *that* could fill several volumes.

"It's kind of hard to explain," I admitted.

And suddenly I realized how much I wanted to. It would be so great if I could get my other friends to see Philomena as I did, to get them to see that her strange vibe was actually one of the best things about her.

Also one of the most frustrating.

"She transferred in this year," Becca reminded me. "So where did she come from?"

"I don't know where she's from. Not exactly.

Whenever I bring it up, she changes the subject. I don't even know if she has a family."

Rebecca frowned. "How could she not have a family? She lives alone, you mean?"

Where *did* Philomena live? I suddenly wondered. How did she spend her time when she wasn't with me? I knew she had a job at a local restaurant. But when she wasn't working or at school, where did she go? She said she had been sent to help me, but was I the only one?

"I'm not sure," I admitted. "I'm not really sure of anything about her."

"Don't you think that's just a little weird?" Rebecca asked. "Doesn't it bother you?"

"I guess I never really thought about where she lives," I answered honestly. "Now that you mention it, it does seem a little odd."

"Well, ask her. Maybe she'll give you a straight answer, and if she won't tell you, maybe we should follow her sometime," Rebecca said.

My jaw practically hit the table it dropped so hard and fast. "*What?*"

"I think we need to try to find out about Philomena," Rebecca explained. "Who she really is, where she lives. Stuff like that."

"You mean, you think we should spy on her. No way."

"Not spy, exactly. But there's just something

about Philomena that makes my spine tingle, Grace. She seems nice, but she's keeping things from us. Maybe she's mixed up with something dangerous.

"Calm down, Becca," I said. "Now *you're* weirding me out. Philomena is not dangerous. She's just different."

How can I explain? I wondered. Dangerous? Hardly. As a matter of fact, Philomena had literally saved my life.

A picture came into my mind. A cold September night. After partying with Dana and her brother. After being humiliated by them, realizing they'd never been my friends. Scared, furious, drunk out of my skull. My absolute low point. I ended up standing in the middle of the highway, daring the cars to run over me.

One of them would have managed it, too, but Philomena showed up. Out of nowhere in her little VW Bug. She claimed she was just passing by. But I knew better. I knew it was more than coincidence, way more.

But I was having a hard time imagining how I could explain all this to Rebecca. Not only that, now that she'd brought up how little we knew about Philomena—where she went, what she did—I realized how much I wanted to know. The truth was, sometimes Philomena's mysteriousness drove me straight up the wall.

"Philomena is my friend. And you don't spy on your friends," I said finally. "I'll talk to her. Really, I will."

"Okay. But if she won't tell you and I see an opportunity to find out, I'm going to take it."

"But—"

"And you might as well admit it, Grace," Rebecca said. "You'll want to come along."

Three

LAST PERIOD OF THE DAY, English class. As I headed to the classroom, all I could think about was hearing the final bell, the signal that I was free to head over to Jackson's house.

I kept imagining what might happen. Were we going to have any one-on-one time? Somehow I didn't think we were just going to discuss the album cover. The possibilities for me and Jackson had been building up for a long time now.

So I definitely was not thinking about *The Great Gatsby*. I hadn't finished the reading assignment, and knew I couldn't fake it if I tried. Which had me hoping Ms. Kaplanski would not ask me about it.

Ms. Kaplanski is one of my favorite teachers. I don't like going to her class unprepared. For one thing, she has a tendency to call on me, whether I put my hand up or not. And for another, ever since I nearly fell apart in September, she had been keeping a close eye on me.

Now she stood at the front of the class, ready to begin just as I slipped into an empty seat next to Rebecca.

"Take out a notebook, everyone," Ms. Kaplanski said.

I felt a churning in my stomach. Surprise quiz. Just my luck.

"We're going to start a creative writing assignment today," Ms. Kaplanski said instead. "One that you'll be finishing up at home. We've been talking about the first-person voice and the role of an unreliable narrator, especially as it appears in *Gatsby*.

"I would like you to use that voice in a short piece, about 500 to 750 words. The completed assignment is due on Friday."

Low groan from the class. Sigh of relief from yours truly. Off the hook on the pop quiz. Thank you, God.

I generally like creative writing. I just need to get in a zone. I didn't mind that assignment at all.

Before we got started, though, Ms. Kaplanski talked some more about "unreliable narrators," listing points on the chalkboard for us to consider.

Basically, she was asking us to write a short story where the narrator was a character who may not be telling the truth—or may only be telling *part* of the truth. Which means that the readers can't fully trust the narrator and always have to piece together the real story themselves.

The assignment struck a chord with me, and I could tell it did with Rebecca, too. There were so many issues of trust floating around lately.

In spite of all the other homework I had going, not to mention my job, I was actually sort of looking forward to writing the story. Maybe I would use it as an opportunity to work out some of my experiences with Philomena. Names changed to protect the innocent, of course.

"Grace," Ms. Kaplanski said, just as I was halfway out the door. "Could I see you for a minute?"

I went over to her desk, wondering if she somehow knew how little time I'd been devoting to my English homework.

"I know you didn't sign up for yearbook this fall," she began.

That was true. Back in September, I could barely get myself to school everyday. I hadn't signed up for any extracurricular activities.

"But I was wondering if I might persuade you to do some caricatures for us," she went on. "You know, the kind of cartoons of students and faculty you did last year. You have a talent for making things funny without insulting anyone."

"Thanks," I said. It would be one more thing to

add to an already overbooked schedule. But I liked drawing for the yearbook, and it felt good to know that Ms. Kaplanski still wanted me to be part of things. "Sure," I said. "I'll see what I can do."

I took the bus home, walked the dog, and then went up to my room to get ready for Jackson's house. My mother was at work, so there were no questions to answer about why I was rushing around, changing my clothes and trying to look good without looking as if I'd been trying too hard.

I had already packed up the artwork I wanted to show Jackson. That was the easy part. It was my outfit that was giving me trouble. Several tries and a small mountain of clothes on the bed later, I studied myself critically in the mirror. Tight-fitting jeans on the bottom, the same ones I had worn to school, with a cream-colored camisole covered by a brown velour hoodie on top.

Perfect, I thought. The fact that I hadn't changed absolutely everything showed I was making an effort, but not too much effort.

Now all I have to do is hope I haven't gone to all this effort for nothing, I told myself. An unsettling thought occurred to me. What if all my friends and I were wrong? What if Jackson didn't really like me? What if I was just projecting, making the whole thing up?

Was I the unreliable narrator of my own (currently nonexistent, but a girl could always hope, couldn't she?) love life?

Give it a rest, Grace, I thought.

I washed my face and brushed my teeth. Then brushed my hair, too. It used to be long, past my shoulders. But I had cut it short in a fit of . . . something . . . the night before school started. It surprised everybody at first, myself included. But now I kind of liked it. It was starting to grow back in, and it had all these interesting layers.

You know. Like me.

I looked at my reflection in the mirror and grinned at the thought.

"*Earrings, Grace,*" I told myself. I grabbed my favorite new pair, silver hoops with small blue beads at the bottom. Then I touched up my lip gloss.

I was ready now. No more putting it off. Suddenly aware that I was nervous, but doing my best to tell myself I wasn't, I headed downstairs and marched bravely toward the front door.

But my fake confidence was totally spoiled when I realized I had forgotten my portfolio. At the rate I was going, band practice would be over before I made it the three blocks to Jackson's house.

Dashing back upstairs, then down again with the portfolio tucked securely under one arm, I grabbed my jean jacket and headed out the door. I was glad the weather was on the cool side.

I definitely needed to chill out.

Though Matt and Jackson had been friends for forever, I had hardly spent any time at the Turners' house. I was usually sitting in the car while Jackson and Matt were running in or out, catching a ride, or getting dropped off.

I reached the house quickly and walked up the path toward the front door. There was a big tree out front, at the side of the property. I remembered how Matt and Jackson had once built a clubhouse there when they were little. I rode over on my bike to see it, but Matt wouldn't let me go up inside and I practically started crying, thinking it was such a big deal.

Jackson had been the nice one, saying it was okay for me to come up, even though Matt got mad at him.

I wasn't sure why I remembered that now.

The driveway was empty and it looked like no one was home. I rang the front doorbell and waited, but didn't hear any sounds inside.

"Hi, Grace." Jackson's younger brother, Sam,

rode up the driveway on his bike, then straight up on the lawn, pulling a wheelie as he came to a stop.

"Hi, Sam. Is Jackson around? I rang the bell but nobody answered."

"He's in there. He's probably just got his headphones on. They're practically an extra appendage."

Even though he's only eleven, Sam talks like this all the time. He loves words. Always has. He even has a notebook where he collects new ones.

He jumped off the bike and dropped it onto the lawn.

"Cool bike," I said. And it was—a low-slung Mongoose, chrome and black, with a trick rod sticking out the back wheel.

Sam flashed a quick smile. "Jackson gave it to me for my birthday."

"Well, that pretty much rules the world," I said.

"It rules the *universe*," Sam said. "Including Pluto, even if it's not a planet anymore."

I laughed, but I was impressed. The bike must have cost at least three hundred dollars. I knew Jackson really wanted to make the CD and was saving money for that, but still, he had been generous enough to buy his brother a really great gift.

Sam pulled a key out of his pocket and opened the front door. "Jaaaackson. Grace is here," he called as we stepped into the foyer.

Jackson appeared on the upstairs landing, an ear

bud hanging out of one side of his head, the wire trailing.

Sam flashed me another grin. "Told you so."

"Grace . . . wow. Is it four-thirty already?" Jackson said. His voice sounded cool, but I saw the way his eyes lit up when he caught sight of me. "Sorry I didn't hear the door."

I shrugged. "That's okay. I wasn't waiting long."

Jackson came down the stairs. He was barefoot, wearing jeans and a wrinkled T-shirt that said, ROCK & ROLL SAVES LIVES. Though his hair was slightly damp, standing up in little spikes as if he'd had a shower, he hadn't shaved and his cheeks and chin were shadowed with stubble.

For a second I just stared at him. I always knew he was cute, but how had I missed the fact that he was *hot*?

"This way to the new music room," he said, and gestured down the hall. I thought I saw a funny expression cross Sam's face. But in the next minute he was heading back out to ride his bike, so it was kind of hard to tell.

"This used to be my dad's study," Jackson said as he went down the hall ahead of me, then opened a door. There was a low leather couch, a glass-topped coffee table, and lots of bookshelves.

"After he left, my mom said I could take it over. She and Sam won't even come in here anymore."

So that explained the look I'd caught on Sam's face.

"My dad left in such a hurry, he left his stereo system behind," Jackson went on. "So now I do my listening in here, but the guys and I still practice in the garage."

"Nice setup," I said, gazing around. I could see why Jackson would want to take this room over, in spite of his dad splitting. The stereo equipment was top of the line.

It was also clearly Jackson's room now. Empty soda cans and candy wrappers littered the floor. Marked-up sheet music was spread out on the coffee table. A crumpled T-shirt poked out from under the couch.

"Here, sit down. I'll make a space." Jackson nudged a stack of guitar magazines off the couch and onto the floor. I sat down, the portfolio on my lap.

"Is that the artwork?" Jackson asked as he settled down beside me.

I nodded. "I brought a whole stack of stuff. I don't expect you to like them all."

"Let's take a look."

I untied the portfolio and lifted out a few of the pieces I'd put on top—the ones I liked the most. Jackson sat next to me and leaned in close. I could feel his leg pressed along the length of mine. He smelled amazing. We sat in silence for a moment as he leafed through my drawings.

Say something, Grace. Say something.

"When are the rest of the guys coming over?"

It sounded like I didn't want to be alone with him when I really did.

Nice job, Grace. Excellent choice.

"Oh, I don't know," Jackson replied. "Should be any time now. We all try to be on time, but . . ." He gave a shrug, and I felt the way his shoulder moved against mine. "Sometimes things get in the way."

As if his words had been a cue, Sam's voice floated through the door. "Jackson, Mom called. She said for you to call her."

"Okay," Jackson called back.

"She said to call her right now," Sam shouted. "She wants to make sure you're really home."

Jackson gave a sigh and rolled his eyes. "My mom is totally freaked about the whole after-school thing," he confided. "She's worried I'm going to not come home when I'm supposed to, or I'll space out and forget Sam's around. As if it's possible to overlook an eleven-year-old."

"Yeah, you think he's such a pain," I teased. "That's why you bought him a new bike."

Jackson's eyes widened in surprise. They're this amazing color, a sort of green mixed with gold. He was sitting so close, I could see each individual gold fleck.

"Did Sam tell you that?" Jackson asked.

I nodded. "He was riding it when I came over. He told me you got it for him, for his birthday. He seems pretty thrilled."

Jackson looked down to where our hands rested, side by side, on top of my portfolio.

"It's really no big deal. I saw a good sale. Sam needs a bike, especially with my mother at work all the time. He rides it to school and out with his friends. His last bike was stolen and my parents are such a mess, fighting over everything, it was pretty clear neither of them was going to step up and get a new one for him."

I could hear the anger in his voice when he talked about his parents.

"Still, it was really nice of you to get it for him," I said. "Particularly when you're trying to save money for making that CD. You put what someone else wanted first. Lots of people can't—or won't—do that."

"Tell me about it," he said, and now his tone was bitter. "Sometimes just thinking about the way my parents are behaving makes me a little crazy. I know everybody says this when things go wrong, but sometimes . . . life is just so unfair."

"I know exactly what you mean," I said. And, of course, I did.

"Right. We both know." Jackson seemed to relax a little. "Thanks, Grace," he said. "It's good to be able to talk this way. To feel like I can be myself. Instead of whatever it is somebody else needs me to be."

"I think you're fine when you're just yourself," I answered.

Omigosh. Had I actually said that?

"I like you, Grace," Jackson said quietly. "Sitting here with you, I might even like myself . . . for the first time in forever."

"That's good," I said. "I like you, too."

That was when I knew it was going to happen. He was going to kiss me. And he did.

Softly at first. Then harder, cupping the back of my head with his hand, pulling me in close. I put my arms around him, held on tight, and kissed him back.

It was nothing like I had imagined. Not that I'm altogether certain what that was. Another movie moment, perhaps. But kissing Jackson was just about the most real thing I've ever done. And so it was better than any fantasy could ever be.

I could feel our bodies pressed together. Feel the edges of his teeth as he nibbled against my lips. Kissing Jackson Turner made me feel . . . important and alive. And it made me want to go on feeling just like that.

The kiss ended and Jackson leaned back. Not too far, just far enough to look into my eyes. I couldn't quite read the expression in his, but I thought I saw a hint of surprise.

I'm not sure what would have happened next. At just that moment, Sam's voice carried through the door.

"Ja-a-a-a-ck-s-o-o-o-n!" he yelled. I think he was standing right outside the room. "It's Mom again. She needs to talk to you. *Right now!*"

Just for a moment, I saw the anger and frustration leap back into Jackson's eyes. Then he just looked tired—and resigned.

"All right, I heard you," he called. "Now do me a favor and get off my back."

"Do me a favor and call Mom!" Sam shouted back, and stomped off down the hall.

Jackson scooted back with a shake of his head. "That settles things," he said. "I'm selling that kid on eBay, first chance I get." He stood up. "I'll be right back. Sorry about this."

"No problem," I replied.

Then he surprised me by handing me his iPod. "You can check out my playlists if you want."

He left the room, closing the door quietly behind him. I sat back with the iPod and took a breath. Then I got up and began to explore the room. I thought it might help to clear my head. Not to mention calm my raging hormones. And yeah, I was curious.

Like the furniture, the rest of the room was this sort of weird hybrid of Jackson's and his dad's stuff. It was clear Jackson intended to take over. There

53

were two electric guitars in stands. He'd hung a bulletin board with photos above his dad's desk, posters on the walls. Some from bands like The Fray and Black Eyed Peas. There was also a really cool one of B. B. King, which he must have picked up at a vintage music store.

I walked a little closer to the desk and studied his pictures.

A few were of Jackson's family. Others were of the Daily Dose playing on stage. There was one of Jackson and Sam, sitting in a cool sports car at a car show. And one of him and Matt, out camping.

I remember that trip, I thought. They had come home reeking because our dog, Wiley, had flushed out a skunk. I laughed, thinking about all the cans of tomato juice Matt went through to get rid of the smell in his fur.

Jackson had a huge collection of CDs, of course, most in high towers as well as some in random stacks on the bookshelves. There was a laptop on the desk and on the very top of the tallest CD tower, a lone stuffed animal. A floppy, almost flat, tiger that looked as if it had been worn out from pure devotion.

I sat down again and put on the ear buds from the iPod. I flicked through his first playlist, looking for a good tune. I didn't have an iPod or an MP3, so I wasn't used to working it. My arm got tangled in the earphone wire and yanked the ear bud out of my ear.

Ouch! I thought, as my hoop earring came right along with it. I heard it *ping* as it hit the hardwood floor.

I disentangled myself from the iPod and got down on my hands and knees to search. The earring wasn't under the couch. Great. With my luck, it could have rolled anywhere. I could just see Jackson returning to find me crawling around on the floor.

I stood up, determined to avoid that humiliation, and a flash of color caught my eye. Sure enough, the earring had rolled over toward the desk, where it had wedged itself between one leg and the trash can that sat alongside.

I bent over to pick it up and found myself staring straight at something that carried the Alternate Realities logo. It looked official. Maybe it had fallen off the desk by mistake. I reached for it.

That's odd, I thought. It was a deposit bag, a long, zippered vinyl pouch that could hold several deposit envelopes at once. That first day at work I had seen Ms. Newberry putting checks, cash, and credit card receipts in one just like it.

What was Jackson doing with a deposit bag at home?

There's a perfectly reasonable explanation, I told myself as I set the deposit bag on the desk.

I knew Jackson was being given more responsibilities at the store. Dave Harper, his department manager, must have asked him to take the deposit to the bank on the way home. It was right on his way. Of course the teller handed the bag back to him after he made the deposit. After that, he'd just come on home, put the deposit bag on the desk, where it got knocked into the garbage without him even noticing.

The room *was* kind of a mess.

"Sorry about that," Jackson said as he came back into the room. "My mom is sort of wired for sound. Nothing seems to convince her that something else bad isn't going to happen the minute she turns her back."

He came toward me, and I moved to meet him. The expression in his face made me forget entirely about my fly-away earring and the mysterious deposit bag.

"Now . . . where were we?" Jackson asked.

In seconds I was back in his arms, and it felt so good—sweet and exciting and as if this was exactly where we were meant to be.

He lowered his mouth to mine for a long, slow kiss—until Sam started pounding on the door again.

"The other guys are here!" he shouted. "They're setting up in the basement and said to tell you to move it!"

Jackson released me with a groan. "Sorry," he said.

"It's okay. I knew you were rehearsing."

He ran a hand lightly down the side of my face. "We've got to do this again," he told me. "When we won't be interrupted every five seconds."

I nodded. My pulse was racing, but I was trying to look cool and composed. "Another time," I agreed.

"So do you want to show the guys your art?" he asked.

Suddenly, I felt transparent. I was sure that the minute the guys in the band saw me, they would know that I was crushing on Jackson, that he and I had been kissing. . . .

"Um . . . we didn't really discuss which of my pieces might work, but why don't you show the guys the portfolio?" I suggested. "I can just leave the whole thing, and you can all look it over and tell me what you want later."

"You're sure you don't want to show it to them yourself?"

"Positive."

"Okay." He nodded. "Tell you the truth, you won't be missing all that much. We sound like crap for about the first two hours of practice, anyway."

I laughed and picked up my jacket. He walked

me to the door, then stood for a moment, hesitating before he opened it. As if, now that the moment was here, he was reluctant to see me go.

"Are you working tomorrow?" he asked.

"Yep. Though I'm not sure what department. What about you?"

"Me, too." Jackson nodded. "I'll be in music. I'll look for you on your break."

"Okay. Sounds good." I hesitated. He still hadn't opened the door.

"I'm glad you came over," he said after a pause. "Maybe there won't be so many interruptions next time."

Next time? I liked the sound of that. It definitely sounded promising. On impulse, I turned toward him. As if he'd just been waiting for some signal from me, Jackson leaned down for a quick kiss.

"Catch you later."

"Yeah, later," I said. I gave his waist a squeeze and pulled open the door. "Have a good practice."

"I will now." He stood at the door and watched me as I headed down the path. I waved and he waved back, then shut the door.

I took a deep breath and dug my hands deep in the pockets of my denim jacket.

Wow.

Me and Jackson. The feeling was mutual, and it

felt just right. I wasn't altogether certain what was going to happen next. But I did know one thing:

I couldn't wait to find out.

That night, as promised, I IM'd my friends and told them the news: Jackson and I were now . . . well, we had kissed. Twice. And planned to do it some more.

Andy congratulated me, Becca wrote, "Way to go, girl!" and Sara sent me a slightly mushy quote from *Romeo and Juliet*. Basically, they approved.

Philomena didn't IM, which was kind of a relief. The truth was: I wasn't sure I wanted to tell her about this. In some ways, Philomena knew me better than just about anyone, even Becca. But somehow, it was hard to imagine talking to her about things like kissing.

The next day at school, all I could think about was seeing Jackson again. It was hard to concentrate on my classes. I kept picturing myself in his music room, kept remembering the feel of our arms around each other. I know it sounds sappy, but I could still hardly believe he felt the same way I did.

But by the time third-period study hall rolled around, I had gone from feeling exhilarated and expectant to let down and grumpy. No matter where I looked, I hadn't caught so much as a glimpse of

Jackson all morning. We hadn't even passed each other in the halls.

So I planted my butt in a seat and pulled out my unreliable-narrator story. It wasn't all that great at providing a distraction. In fact, I wasn't doing any writing at all, just doodling in my notebook. On impulse, I put away my English notebook and pulled out my sketchbook. An idea popped into my head for the CD cover for the band.

This happens to me sometimes. I'm doing one thing—like studying or even taking a shower—and all of a sudden, an idea for a drawing pops into my brain. I've learned that I have to get it down while it's fresh or it will fade away and I'll lose it forever.

This time it wasn't so tough. At least I wasn't in the shower. I was making a rough sketch with a regular pencil, when I felt someone staring down over my shoulder. My whole body flushed with a sudden warmth. For no logical reason, I felt better than I had all day.

I didn't need to turn around to know who was there.

Philomena.

"Hi, Phil," I said, then glanced back. "What's up?"

"How did you know it was me?" she asked, smiling. "I didn't want to break your concentration. I was trying to be quiet."

"You were quiet," I said. "I just . . . sensed you were back there, that's all."

She came a step closer and looked down at the pad. "What are you working on?"

"Jackson asked if I could do a sketch for the Daily Dose. They're going to cut a CD and need some art for the cover."

Philomena's eyes widened. "Wow, that's cool." She sat down in the seat next to me. "When did all this happen?"

"Yesterday, mostly. And the day before."

"Sounds like you've been seeing a lot of Jackson."

"Yeah," I said happily. "I think we finally got past having all that . . . awkwardness . . . between us."

"That's good," she said, and I felt that wave of warmth from her again. "That means you're really letting go of some of the anger over Matt's death."

I nodded. "Yeah. I know it wasn't Jackson's fault. And that lets me see what an amazing guy he really is. I'm glad Jackson wasn't hurt. I know now he had nothing to do with why Matt died."

One of Philomena's eyebrows lifted. "That is a major change of attitude, Grace."

I shrugged, feeling a bit embarrassed. "Well, I'm finally getting to know him. He works at Alternate Realities, too." I shot her a look. "But then, you already know that, don't you?"

She cocked her head, as if she was puzzled. "I do?"

"Come on, Philomena," I said. "I know you were helping me get a job to repay my parents, but I figured out why you picked Alternate Realities. It's because Jackson works there, and he and I—we were meant to get together."

Philomena gave me one of her unreadable looks. "Were you?"

"Yes," I said. "What? You think I'm supposed to be helping Ms. Newberry? Well, why can't I do that *and* be friends with Jackson? Isn't friendship important, too?" I felt dishonest even as I asked the question; I wanted to be a lot more than friends with Jackson.

I waited for Philomena to call me on it, but all she said was, "Of course. It's just . . . I'd hate to see you get hurt all over again."

"What are you talking about?" I demanded. I started drawing again, shading in a section of the drawing with the flat side of my pencil, pressing hard as if for extra emphasis. "Why should I get hurt? Jackson's a great guy."

Ms. Nagy, the study hall teacher, glanced up from the papers she was marking. "Stanley, the rule is you can talk in here but quietly. Got it?"

"Got it," I said.

Philomena reached out and touched my arm.

"Jackson *is* a great guy," she said softly. "But you two have very complicated ties, and that can make what happens between you hard to read sometimes. And you feel . . . close to him, don't you? Not just because of Matt. Because you have feelings of your own. You have for quite a while now."

I stopped drawing. I wasn't in the mood anymore.

"You don't think I should go out with him, do you?"

"It's not my place to tell you—"

"You're right," I said. "It's not. This is between Jackson and me." I caught myself. I didn't want to snap at Philomena. I tried again. "Jackson and I really understand each other. We're both missing Matt," I explained. "Being with him makes me happy. I thought you would be happy for me."

Philomena was really quiet. Then she sighed and said, "I do want you to be happy, Grace," she said. "I suppose . . . I just see things differently."

"What do you see?" I snapped. "Why can't you ever just say what you mean? Why can't I get a straight answer out of you? Why do you always have to be so . . . so mysterious? I don't even know where you live!"

"Stanley," Ms. Nagy said, "you can either lower your voice or return here at the end of the day for detention. Which is it going to be?"

"I'd better go," Philomena said. "See you later, okay?"

"Can't wait," I muttered.

I watched her walk off, long hair swaying gently as she moved. Philomena might be walking away, but I had a feeling the discussion was far from over.

Four

"**Gracious, Grace!**" Ms. Newberry exclaimed as I dashed through Alternate Realities' front door, the bells chiming madly overhead. "You look like you've been shot out of a canon. I'm not sure that's really the best energy to bring into the store."

"I'm sorry, Ms. Newberry," I apologized. "The bus was slow and I didn't want to be late."

Today she was wearing a long blue dress decorated in a pattern that reminded me of puffy white clouds. A trailing white scarf around her neck completed the look.

"A few minutes here or there doesn't make a big difference to me," Ms. Newberry said. "Not that I want you to make a habit of being late, of course. But stress puts a strain on your entire system. It creates toxins and oxidants. You don't need those, and neither do our customers. Now . . ."

She did that head-tilt thing again, her eyes studying me closely. "A blue apron again today, I think."

All of a sudden, her brown eyes began to twinkle. "Think serene thoughts while you put it on."

"Right," I said. I went for the apron, wondering again if the person I was supposed to help was Ms. Newberry. In her own strange kind of way, she seemed so sane that it was hard to see where she might need help. Except with things like falling dishes, of course.

Apparently, Jackson wasn't the only one who approved of the way I stacked plates. Ms. Newberry had me spend most of my second day right back in the Embellishments department. A brand new shipment of dishes from Italy had just come in, painted with these elaborate bird and flower motifs. I had to admit they were pretty gorgeous.

It was nearly five o'clock before I got a break. One of the perks of being an Alternate Realities staffer was that if you stayed beneath a certain dollar limit, you could have free food on your break. I went to the cooler in the back of the store and snagged a bottle of papaya juice and a bag of whole grain chips.

Secretly, I was hoping Jackson might have a break at the same time—and he did.

"Grace," I heard him say. "Hi."

Thank you, God, I thought. Then hoped He wouldn't think less of me for thanking Him for something that was only important to me. And Jackson, too, of course. But we weren't exactly talking world peace here.

"Hi, yourself," I said. "You on break, too?"

He nodded. "Uh-huh. You went for those chips, too. They're not bad for something ridiculously healthy." He walked over, snagged himself a bag and a bottle of raspberry-flavored mineral water.

"I showed the rest of the band your artwork," he said as he sat down.

One of the girls who works in the clothing department, STACY her name tag said, came in. Both Jackson and I gave a nod. But I was secretly relieved when she grabbed her jacket and headed out.

"And?" I said, suddenly nervous.

"They liked it," Jackson said. He popped a handful of chips into his mouth. "They liked it a lot." He gave a sudden, lopsided grin. "Even Charlie."

"Well, that rocks," I said. "I've been doing some more thinking—does the CD have a theme or a title?"

"Not really," Jackson shook his head. He scooted his chair a little closer, and I swear I felt my whole body grow warm. We were just sitting in the break room talking, but it felt so good to be close to him. The more time I spent with Jackson, the more I realized how long I had wanted something like this to happen.

Wanted him to notice me. To think of me as something more than his best friend's little sister.

Wanted him to want me.

"The CD is really sort of an introduction. A way of showing what we can do," he went on. "Since all the bands at the competition will be selling them, I want ours to have really cool artwork. It'll help us stand out, get noticed."

"That and how excellent the band sounds," I said.

Jackson smiled, his whole face lighting up. Without warning, he reached out and caught the fingers of my right hand, linking them with his own.

"That, too, of course."

"I did another sketch yesterday," I said. He was running his thumb along the back of my hand, sending delicious little tingles up and down my spine. "In study hall. Charlie will be happy. It features a car."

Jackson gave a chuckle. He reached into his bag of chips, took a couple out. He lifted his eyebrows as if in question. I nodded, and he popped them in my mouth. It's kind of amazing I was able to chew and swallow. The brush of his fingertips against my lips made my entire body want to seriously malfunction.

"I was thinking maybe the cover could be a drawing of a car—funky—big fat lines, like maybe a kid's drawing. A convertible, with you guys inside. Your bodies could be this cool collage technique I just learned. I could Photoshop in your actual heads."

Jackson's eyebrows rose. "Our *actual* heads?"

I rolled my eyes. "Photos of your actual heads," I said. "Though I might make an exception in your case."

"I'm scared now."

"You should be," I teased. "I know you haven't really decided on a title, but . . . what would you think about *Joy Ride*? That would tie in to the image, but it's general enough to cover whatever cuts you wanted."

I took a breath. This next part could get a little hard. "Plus, I was thinking," I went on. "It might— you know. Sort of a play on words. You were saying you wanted the CD to celebrate Matt's music." My voice trailed off.

"I think that's perfect," Jackson said. "And I think you're amazing, Grace." He leaned closer then, unmistakable intent in his eyes.

He's going to kiss me, I thought. *Right here in the break room.*

"Oh, Grace. Good," I suddenly heard Ms. Newberry's voice as she appeared in the doorway. "I was hoping you hadn't gone out. I'm sorry to cut your break a little short, but we just got a sudden rush and . . ."

"I'll be right there." I stood up quickly, then realized Jackson still had my hand.

"Thank you, dear," Ms. Newberry said, turning and bustling back out onto the sales floor, her long skirt flowing out behind her.

I shot Jackson a panicked look. "Do you think she saw?"

"Saw what? Us holding hands?"

Before I quite realized what he intended, Jackson gave my hand a tug. I leaned forward and he gave me a quick kiss, then let me go.

"See you after work," he said. As if he was already planning on us walking home together.

"Okay, see you," I said, unable to keep from smiling.

No two ways about it: I was seriously going to like this job.

The rest of my shift went quickly. Once the late-afternoon rush was over, Ms. Newberry asked me to help her change the display in the front window. My first mission: to scour the store for items that could be used to illustrate an autumn harvest theme.

I have to admit I really got into it. When Matt and I were little, my parents always used to take us to the big state fair. Next to the animals, the thing we loved the most were the grange displays—sort of mosaics made up of jars of homemade pickles and preserves, fresh fruits and vegetables, and heaps of colorful dried beans, all arranged together to form a visual theme.

One year the theme was something like "Westward Ho!" In my favorite display, all the stuff was arranged in the shape of a covered wagon. Dozens of eggs made up the white canvas top. I totally loved it.

Before I even realized what I was doing, I had turned the front window of AR into a sort of world-wide grange display. Ms. Newberry was completely impressed.

"You have a real eye for this sort of thing, Grace," she said. "Now that I know you enjoy doing it, we'll have to talk about having you take on some of the cash register displays. The music department is due for a big changeover soon, I think."

The *music department,* I thought. *How about that?*

"Next time you come in, wear a lavender apron," Ms. Newberry suggested. "It boosts creativity."

"Lavender? Okay." I nodded. "I'll remember that."

Ms. Newberry checked her watch. "It's a little early, but why don't you just go on home? Go ahead and write down hours for your full shift."

"That would be great. Thanks, Ms. Newberry," I said.

I headed for the back room, took off my apron, grabbed my stuff, then did what I sincerely hoped was a casual stroll on over to the music department. It had been a while since I'd been interested in looking at music. Really, not since Matt died. Today, though, I figured I could check out new CDs while I waited for Jackson to get off.

Dave Harper, the department manager, was on the floor helping a customer. But I didn't see Jackson anywhere. *Maybe Dave sent him to the back,* I thought. *To do a restock.* Then I remembered I had just come from the back room and hadn't seen him anywhere.

That's odd, I thought.

Generally speaking, AR employees stayed in their own departments. It wasn't unheard of for them to rove around, but Ms. Newberry liked people to have a specialty and really get to know a particular area of the store. So working in more than one area at once didn't happen all that often.

A second customer materialized at the cash register, clearly ready to be rung up. I saw Dave Harper glance around the department. I was pretty sure he was looking for Jackson. A second later I saw Dave excuse himself from the customer he was helping and move to the register. He was looking annoyed now.

Jackson, where are you? I thought. All of a sudden, finding him seemed incredibly important. Dave having to wait on two customers at once might not seem like a big deal in the overall scope of things, but Ms. Newberry prided herself on excellent customer service. Besides that, Dave looked angry, and I knew Jackson wouldn't want to get on the wrong side of his boss.

He couldn't afford to screw up. He really needed this job.

I walked out of the music department, hoping I still looked casual. Secretly, my senses were on full alert in "find-Jackson" mode. I walked down the main aisle, casting quick glances left and right.

There he is! I thought in relief. Over in the poster and card department. He was just closing the cash register drawer. I saw him glance around. Then he made a quick movement, like he was stuffing something in his pants pocket. It was over so fast I almost wasn't certain I'd actually seen it happen.

"Jackson," I said in a low voice.

He jumped, then spun toward me. His face was flushed.

"Grace," he said. "What are you doing in this department?"

"Looking for you," I said. "Look, I just came from music. Dave's waiting on a bunch of customers and I think he's getting seriously annoyed. He keeps looking around like he's wondering where you are."

Jackson's expression changed—as if he were frightened and trying not to show it.

"Thanks for the heads up," he said. "I shouldn't be too long. Maybe you could wait for me out front?"

"Okay, sure," I said. *It's November,* I thought. A little cold to wait around outside. Something Jackson would have realized if he had been thinking clearly. Which he obviously wasn't.

What's going on? I wondered.

"See you in a few," Jackson said. He took off for the music department at a brisk walk. Much more slowly, I walked toward AR's front door. With every step I took, I felt my supergood mood of the day slip a little.

Was there something going on? Or was my overactive imagination just making things up? I was so excited about the turn my relationship with Jackson was taking. Was I indulging in some weird psychological sabotage? Looking for things to go wrong?

Whoa, Grace, I thought. *Wait a minute. Slow down.* I hadn't actually seen Jackson *do* anything, let alone do anything wrong. It was all what the TV cop shows would call circumstantial evidence at this point. That and my own gut feeling.

It was true that my romantic feelings for Jackson were a pretty recent development. But I'd known him most of my life. And I thought that meant I knew him well enough to spot when he was acting out of character.

Like, for instance, now.

Of course, the divorce was putting him under a lot of pressure. He'd told me that himself.

I pushed open the front door of AR, stepping out into a cold, clear November night. I thought I could catch just the hint of smoke on the air, even on Main Street. As if somewhere somebody had a bonfire going, maybe burning leaves.

I loitered in front of the display window I had just put in. It made the whole store look warm and inviting. Ms. Newberry was already talking about putting in a Thanksgiving window, featuring vegetarian options to the traditional meal. Now that was going to be a challenge.

"Hey, Grace," Jackson came out the door fast, as if glad to be out of the building. "Thanks for waiting. Sorry, I didn't think about the cold."

"That's all right," I said.

He reached for my hand, giving it a quick squeeze before linking his fingers through mine and thrusting our joined hands into his coat pocket. I felt my heart rate bump up a notch, even as my stomach plummeted.

His jacket was new. One I had never seen before. An incredibly cool bomber-style jacket made of thick, supple leather. I didn't even want to think about how much it cost.

Where did you get the money for a new jacket, Jackson? I wondered. Where had he gotten the money to pay for Sam's bike? Alternate Realities paid better than some other after-school jobs, but I didn't think it was enough to cover the cost of high-end items like leather jackets and Mongoose bikes.

I can't believe this is happening, I thought.

I'd had a crush on Jackson for practically forever. At last, things between us were moving forward on the personal front. Now, everywhere I looked, weird roadblocks were springing up.

I wanted to ignore them.

I couldn't.

I could not get the weird way Jackson had acted that afternoon out of my mind. And then there was the deposit envelope I'd found in his house.

"Ms. Newberry seems to really like you," Jackson said as we crossed the street and headed for our neighborhood.

We were walking quickly to keep warm. The stores and businesses of Main Street would be behind us in just a few more blocks. At the rate we were going, it wouldn't take us long to get home.

You have to know, Grace, I told myself. *You have to find out what's going on.*

"I like her, too," I answered.

I was just trying to keep the conversation flowing until I figured out a way to approach Jackson about all the weird fears that were floating through my mind. But, as I spoke, I realized how much I meant what I said. I did like Ms. Newberry.

"Not that I intend to start copying her fashion choices."

Jackson smiled.

"But there's something about her . . . she looks for the positive, I guess. The good in people. I think that's nice. You don't meet people like her all that often."

"You're right," Jackson answered quietly.

Was it just my imagination, or had his hold on my hand tightened? *Come on, Grace,* I thought. We didn't have far to go now—just a few more blocks, and once we were at my house, my chance to ask him would be gone.

I took a deep breath. "There is a potential downside to all that, of course."

Jackson's head swiveled toward me. "Like what?"

"Well," I answered carefully. "Someone like that, who wants to see the good, might be easy to take advantage of."

I saw him flush. I know I did. Even though it was pretty dark.

"What makes you say a thing like that?" Jackson asked. I couldn't read the sound of his voice.

"Jackson." I hesitated, summoning my courage. And then I went for it. "I . . . I don't want to say this. I don't even want to think it, but I saw you by the cash register in the art department. And the other day, when I was at your house, in your music room, I lost one of my earrings. And when I was looking for it, I found an AR deposit envelope under the desk. Now you and Sam both have all these new things . . ." Feeling utterly miserable, I let my voice trail off.

Jackson dropped my hand, stuffing his fists into his jacket pockets. I felt the cold again. The wind was whipping through the trees overhead, making them sound like the ocean.

"Life sucks sometimes, doesn't it?" Jackson said. He began to talk fast, the words tumbling over one another. "I mean, currently, mine is so unbelievably messed up. You know I might not even be able to go away to school now, because of the divorce? My mom dropped that bombshell just last night. I might have to go to a community college where they don't even have a decent music program.

"Sometimes I feel like my parents are screwing up my whole life. I wish they would just get divorced already and get over it. Then at least Sam and I would know where we stand. Though actually—"

He gave a bitter laugh. "Who am I kidding? We already know. We're screwed. There's no money for anything, at least not anything that's important to us. That's why I wanted to get him that bike so much."

"Jackson," I said, totally at a loss.

Here was a new question, one as hard to answer as the one about whether or not I was responsible for Matt's accident by helping to put him in the wrong place at the worst possible time. If you do the wrong thing for a good reason—a right reason—does that make it any less wrong? If Jackson stole the money to buy Sam that bike, did that make his action less of a crime? Did it make a difference that he'd also purchased something for himself?

"You want to know if I took money from the store to get stuff Sam and I really needed? Well, maybe I did. But I swear, it was only for a little while. I paid it all back, Grace. Every single penny. It wasn't stealing. Not really. It was more like a loan."

One Ms. Newberry didn't know she was making, I thought. Though I kept that to myself.

"I'm not a bad person. You know that, Grace," Jackson went on. "It's just that some really bad things are happening in my life. I'm just trying to take care of myself and Sam. Because obviously my parents don't even notice that we still exist."

"I'm sorry, Jackson," I said. Never had the words sounded so lame. "I didn't realize things were so bad. I hope they get better for you."

"They will if I make them," he said in a determined voice. He turned toward me, and I could see that same determination in his eyes.

All of a sudden, I realized we had entirely missed the place where he peeled off to his house. We were standing on the sidewalk in front of my house. I thought I saw my mom glance out the living room window, then move away.

Jackson looked down at me, his eyes searching mine. "All sorts of things in my life are weird and stupid right now. You're the one thing that isn't, Grace. You and what's happening with the band are the only things that are going right.

"I did something wrong. I know it, and I'm sorry. But I swear I've already made it right. I put all the money back. I'll never do it again, I promise."

So *that's* what I had just seen him doing—putting the money *back,* not taking more out. I felt the pain I'd felt when I'd believed I couldn't trust him suddenly ease.

He put his hands on my shoulders, leaned in close. "Tell me I haven't screwed us up. Tell me you believe in me, Grace."

"I do believe in you," I said.

I saw the relief flash into his eyes . . . just before he closed the distance and gave me a kiss. Long and slow. Filled with promises. I put my arms around him, no longer caring whether or not my mom might be watching.

Slowly, like coming out of a dream, the kiss ended. When it was over, Jackson rested his forehead against mine.

"I guess you'd better go in, huh?"

"I guess." My heart was beating really fast, trying to keep up with my mind.

I liked Jackson. I liked him so much. I wanted to help make everything right.

Maybe this is the real reason I ended up working at Alternate Realities, I thought. Philomena said I was going to start helping people. Maybe it had never been about Ms. Newberry. Maybe Jackson was the person I was supposed to help all along.

"I'll see you tomorrow," I said.

"Right," he said, as he took a step back. "Say hi to your folks."

"I will," I promised.

I stood on the front porch, watching him walk away. Then I went into my house, hoping I could make it upstairs unnoticed. I needed some time alone in my room to sort out my thoughts.

I hadn't even gotten my coat off when my mother appeared in the hallway.

"Grace? It's about time you got home. We've been waiting. Wash up and come sit down. Dinner's ready."

I dumped my backpack at the foot of the stairs, then washed my hands and splashed my face with cold water in the downstairs bathroom.

When I came into the kitchen, my father was sitting at the table, sifting through the mail. My mother stood at the stove, but turned as I came in.

"How come you're so late, honey? Did you have to work late at the store?"

"I helped Ms. Newberry with the window display."

Technically not a lie. Not a complete answer to her question, either, though.

"You must have taken the long route home. It's nearly seven. We didn't know what happened. We were worried."

My father glanced at my mother, then back at me. Ever since Matt died, both my parents are what I would call time sensitive. If I'm so much as five minutes late, they have a tendency to freak out.

Luckily, they seemed to take turns about it.

"Just call us if you need to stay late at the store, Grace. That's all." My dad gathered his mail in a neat pile and set it on the sideboard.

"Was that Jackson Turner walking with you?" my mother asked. "I wasn't spying," she went on quickly, as if she thought I might accuse her of doing just that. "I just looked out the window."

"Jackson works at AR, too, in the music department. So we walked back from town together."

"How is Jackson? I haven't seen him lately." My father's tone was remarkably normal.

In fact, if someone who didn't know what had happened had heard him, they never would have guessed at Jackson's very loaded history with our family. But I could hear the catch in my dad's voice as he struggled for that "I'm-okay-about-it" voice.

I knew my mother felt it, too. Her fingers were white where she gripped the spoon.

"Actually, things are kind of tough for him," I said. "His folks are splitting up. I think it's hard on him and Sam."

"A divorce?" My mother took the pan off the heat and glanced at my father. "That's too bad. I had no idea."

"Poor Jackson. He's had a tough year." My dad shook his head, looking genuinely concerned for Matt's old friend.

My father's always been a nice guy who doesn't complain or talk badly about other people; he tries to be there for his friends and family. But ever since Matt died, the problems of other people, even strangers, seemed to hit him much deeper. He seemed more aware of people's feelings, whatever hardship they might be going through. I guess he still hurt so much himself that these stories make him identify, connect.

Maybe we've all changed in that way.

"Jackson's hard times just seem to keep coming. First the car accident and now his family breaking up . . ."

Dad's voice trailed off as he shook his head.

I knew all this. Better than anyone. But when my dad said it out loud, it somehow hit home, and the stealing problem seemed to make more sense, fit into context more. It didn't excuse it, but I could see that Jackson had been under so much pressure. He had made some bad choices, just like yours truly, not so very long ago.

"He's a good kid," my father said after a moment. "I hope things turn around for him."

My mother agreed, nodding her head sympathetically. She put the food on the table and we all sat down to eat. I sensed that my parents had said as much as they were able to about Jackson. I think we all felt relieved when my father changed the subject to something going on at work.

I only half listened to my dad's story, feeling the weight of Jackson's secret like a stone, lodging somewhere near my heart. It was a lot to hold inside, a lot to keep to myself. I wished there were someone I could tell.

You could tell Philomena, I thought. In fact, I probably ought to. If there was one person who could help me sort through this mess, it was Philomena.

But the truth was, I didn't want to tell her. Phil had made it pretty clear that she didn't think me going out with Jackson was a good idea.

If I went to her with this, I had a feeling she would tell me that Jackson was trouble, that what I needed to do was to get distance from him. And distance from him was the last thing I wanted.

Jackson's the one I'm supposed to help, I decided. *And I'm going to figure out a way to help him, on my own.*

Five

"**THIS YEAR I AM SO GOING** to win a prize," Rebecca said as she locked the door on her mom's car. It was Saturday afternoon, and Rebecca had driven me and Andy to the school's annual fair. Sara, who was working in the drama club's booth, had gotten there earlier that morning.

"You always win prizes," Andy told Rebecca as we crossed the parking lot to the athletics field. "Remember that awful chartreuse squid you won last year bopping the chipmunk?"

"I won an octopus," Rebecca said patiently, "and the game is Whack-a-Mole."

"Whatever," Andy said. "All those games take too much hand-eye coordination. I think this year I'm just going to give them my money and then go find the cotton candy. It's so much easier that way. No lines, no embarrassing yourself in front of the whole school . . . What about you, Grace?"

I shrugged. "I might play a few games . . ."

The booths were spread out across the athletics field, right next to the track and bleachers. Fortunately, the weather was sunny even though it felt chilly. The place was already jammed with kids from school and families from town who had come to support the cause.

"So, what do we want to do first?" Rebecca looked around, getting her bearings. We all knew it wasn't about playing the games, or even eating that special kind of junk food you can only find at fairs— like cotton candy and funnel cake. It was about seeing everyone else, and being seen. And, in Rebecca's case, anyway, I had a feeling it was about a Scott Hammond sighting.

"Should we go find Sara?" Andy asked. "I think she's at some water-gun thing."

"Sure, let's tell her we're here. Maybe she can take a break and hang with us." Rebecca glanced over my shoulder and her eyebrows shot up.

"What?" I said.

She reached out and seized me by the arm. "It's Scott," she hissed. "Don't turn around! I don't want him to see me looking at him!"

"You're facing his direction, Becca," Andy said, straightforward and practical as always. "So take a deep breath and calm down."

"You're right. I know you're right," Rebecca said. "It's just . . . oh, *no!*"

I did turn around then, just in time to spot Dana Sloan and company cruise up to a booth just a few feet behind us. Scott, who was running the booth, stood behind the wooden counter and sign that read: WHACK-A-MOLE—5 TICKETS.

I could tell from the way Lindsay Wexler was laughing, like a girl in a toothpaste ad—whitest teeth, freshest breath—that the cute, little plastic moles were not the booth's top draw. That would be Scott.

I wonder why Lindsay wants him, I thought. Not that Scott wasn't cute. But he was more low-key than the guys she usually went after.

"Want to come back later? When the crowd clears?" I asked Becca.

She considered my question. Then took a breath and squared her shoulders, the way she does on the lacrosse field. Rebecca is an awesome halfback. The coach calls her The Wall. Now she had that same gleam in her eyes as when the entire opposing team is stampeding toward her and she's all that stands between them and the goal.

"No. Let's play," she said.

"Go for it, Becca!" Andy cheered her on.

We walked up to the booth. Dana and Morgan weren't playing, just hanging around Lindsay, helping her flirt with Scott.

Scott was setting up a board for Lindsay. She was

really pouring it on, acting as if she had no idea how to attack a poor defenseless creature. Which was so far from the truth.

She swung her mallet wildly and giggled. "Don't start yet, I'm not ready."

"You have to hit straight down," Scott said, giving her a quick demo.

Becca stood beside me, sort of bobbing up and down on the balls of her feet, waiting for Scott to notice her.

"Can we play this round?" I asked out loud.

Scott looked up. "No problem. Jump right in." He walked over to take our tickets, giving Becca a smile.

I glanced at Dana. "Hi, Dana. What's up?"

"Just hanging out. What do you say? You guys going to give us a little competition?"

Lindsay looked up. "They hope." Her gaze singled out Rebecca. "You're not going to use your lacrosse stick, are you? That wouldn't be fair, now." She waggled a finger, making her friends laugh.

"I don't think she's carrying it. For once." Dana observed.

Lindsay leaned back, her eyes giving Rebecca the once-over, as if sizing up the competition.

"Nice sweater, Rebecca," she remarked. "What'd you do, find it at the Salvation Army?"

Rebecca was wearing one of the big, baggy

sweaters she borrows from her older brothers—
a teal blue V-neck—over a white tank top.

Dana laughed at Lindsay's remark, and Becca's
face turned scarlet. She has a redhead's coloring;
with fair skin, a sprinkling of freckles; and dark,
curly reddish-brown hair. For a second, I thought she
might turn and run.

But Becca just picked up her mallet and said,
"Ready?"

Scott started the game and the four of us began
whacking away at our boards. The truth is, I was just
playing to keep Rebecca company. Rebecca, however, was playing to win and doing a pretty amazing
job of it.

Scott stood by watching. "Not bad," he said, smiling at her.

"Scott . . . help! I think my mole got stuck," Lindsay cried. "I whacked him but he won't go down."

The buzzer rang then. I had fifty-three points on
my scoreboard, Dana had a few more, Lindsay had
seventy-five, and Rebecca had about a million.

"We have a winner here," Andy shouted, pointing
at Rebecca.

"That's not fair. My mole got stuck!" Lindsay
complained.

"It wasn't really fair. You should play the game
over," Dana added.

"Oh, please," Andy muttered.

"You can have a free game, if you like," Scott offered. His tone was friendly, but . . . maybe it was just my imagination, was it also a little cool? As if he might be the one guy at Warren G. Harding High immune to Lindsay Wexler's charms?

He turned to Rebecca. "Pick out a prize. You had the high score."

"No . . . that's okay." Rebecca said, suddenly shy.

"It isn't okay," Scott insisted. "You should take a prize. You deserve it. Here, I'll even pick it out."

He turned to face the row of prizes, reaching without hesitation for the largest one. A big pink bear with this enormous bow tied around its neck.

"Here," he said, tugging down the stuffed bear and handing it to Rebecca. "Everyone likes bears, right?"

Way to go, Becca, I thought. She had definitely gotten Scott's attention. And literally right under Lindsay's nose.

"Gee . . . thanks." Rebecca took the bear, looking sort of stunned, as if Scott had just handed her a dozen roses.

"No problem. Catch you later, okay?"

"Okay. See you," Rebecca said. But she didn't move a muscle until Andy gave her a gentle tug, pulling her back down to earth.

"Let's go find Sara," I said. "She must be wondering where we are."

We started toward the drama club booth on the other side of the field. Rebecca was walking on air the whole way.

"He said, 'Catch you later.' Do you think that means he's going to look for me? I mean, you know, specifically? Because people say 'Catch you later' all the time. And sometimes they mean—I'll be looking for you later and hope you're looking for me—and sometimes they say it just to have something to say. So which do you suppose it is?"

"I suppose," Andy said, "that only time will tell. But judging by the looks on Lindsay's and Dana's faces, my money's on you, girl."

We found Sara at the drama booth, running a water-pistol contest.

"Perfect timing!" she said when she saw us. "I was just about to go on break."

Sara had barely stepped out of the booth before Rebecca launched into an explanation of why she was carrying a large pink bear.

Sara gave Becca a high five. "Way to go. Those girls are evil. They can't win all the time."

Everyone was hungry, so we headed toward the food booths, at the far end of the fair. We were about halfway there when Sara caught my arm.

"Wait a second . . . is that Jackson?"

I turned to follow her gaze.

Jackson was working in the Pie Toss booth, run

by the varsity baseball team. He wasn't a big athlete but went out for baseball in the spring. He was a pitcher, I recalled, and a pretty good one. Matt had been on the team, too, playing first base. He would have been a starter this year, but I didn't want to think about that.

Jackson was taking a few hits for the team. Up on a stool behind the counter, far enough from the contestants to make it interesting but close enough to get hit, he sat teasing and taunting, ducking and dodging, making all kinds of funny faces while kids took turns flinging pies at him.

We walked closer to get a better look. The pies were only shaving cream enhanced with food coloring, but still, they made a nice mess.

"Give me a break. My grandma can throw better than that," I heard Jackson taunt.

The pie flew and he bent forward, ducking it neatly and making everyone laugh.

"Okay," I said. "I have got to try this."

"Some girls will do anything for attention," Becca said with a smile.

I leaned over and tweaked the pink bear on the ear. "Some girls ought to know."

I paid the guy running the booth and he lined up three pies on the counter for me: pink, yellow, and blue.

When I stepped up to take aim, Jackson's eyes widened.

I loved the shocked expression on his face. He obviously hadn't noticed me standing back in the crowd. He really was so cute, sitting up there. I almost didn't have the heart to slam him with the pies.

Almost.

"Geez! Who let her in?" he cried out when he saw me heft the first one. "Save me, somebody . . . I'm in real trouble now!"

"I'll say you are. You are dead meat, dude." I reared back and got ready to throw.

"Good-bye, cruel world!" he moaned. All around me, I heard the crowd laughing. Jackson knew how to put on a show.

He put his hands over his eyes then parted two fingers to peek out a crack. I let the first pie fly. I thought for sure it was going to hit him. At the very last second, he dodged to one side.

Quickly, before he could even sit up, I hefted the second pie, tossing it with all my might. This time, I was too fast. It sailed right by him.

He gave me a wicked grin, eyes dancing with mischief as he settled himself more firmly on his stool.

"Good try, Grace," he said. "Another six years and you'll just about get the hang of—"

"—it," I finished for him.

Jackson was now incapable of coherent speech, his face covered with blue shaving foam. While he was gloating over my lack of accuracy, I had snuck the other pie behind my back, then quickly turned and let it fly.

Splat!

Direct hit, right in the face.

While the crowd laughed, Jackson sat spluttering and spitting out shaving cream. Theatrically, he scooped it away from his eyes, then, laughing, wiped his face with a towel and smoothed the cream out of his hair, deliberately making it stick up in funny little peaks.

"Good shot, Stanley," he admitted. "Enjoy your prize."

"I already am." I grinned at him.

"Oh yeah?" Jackson jumped down from the high stool and came straight toward me. At the last second, I realized what he intended to do.

"Oh no," I cried, as I tried to step back. "Don't you dare."

"Hey," he said. "One good prize deserves another."

Before I could escape, he grabbed me, pulling me forward into his arms. He planted a great big shaving cream kiss right on my mouth. All around us, the crowd clapped and cheered.

"Eewww," I said, when it was finally over. "That stuff is totally disgusting."

"Tell me about it," Jackson said. He was grinning from ear to ear, and I had a feeling my expression wasn't any more subtle.

"I'm going to remember this, Stanley," he said.

"I hope so," I said, then added more quietly, "I will, too."

He leaned down for another quick kiss, then sauntered back toward the stool.

Oh, well, I thought, still in a happy daze. It looked like our relationship had just gone public.

I cleaned off the shaving cream and we finally headed for the food booths. I was starved. Pie flinging had given me an appetite and everything smelled good, even food I would normally never eat. We split up to make our selections. I filled a cardboard tray with curly fries covered with nacho cheese and a chili dog.

If Ms. Newberry ever saw me pigging out on this stuff, she would have a heart attack. Or fire me. Or both.

But it seemed the perfect day for some seriously unhealthy eating. I met up again with my friends, all carrying trays laden with equally bad food. Except Andy, of course, who couldn't find anything up to her standards except an apple and a carton of milk.

We spotted an empty table and staked a claim.

Just as we were sitting down, Philomena walked by. "Hey, guys . . . can I sit with you?"

"Sure, have a seat." I shifted over to make room.

Phil set down her tray, which held a slice of pizza and a bottle of water, then sat down next to me.

"Are any of you working at the fair today?" she asked.

"I'm at the water-pistol game," Sara said. "For the drama club."

"The rest of us are just hanging out," I added.

"Making sports history," Andy said. "Grace hit Jackson Turner in the face with a pie. It was a classic moment."

Philomena met my eye. "Good way to get his attention," she commented.

The rest of my friends laughed.

I hadn't seen Philomena since we had that fight in study hall. I'd been wondering if she was mad at me.

"How's it going at the yearbook booth?" Rebecca asked Phil.

"Good." Philomena nodded, taking a bite of her pizza. "My shift is over, though. I was there all morning." She smiled at Rebecca's bear. "That's amazing. Where did you win that?"

The simple question was all the encouragement Rebecca needed to relive her moment of glory. She even admitted to Philomena that she liked Scott Hammond. I was sort of surprised. Rebecca had seemed so uncertain, maybe even suspicious of Phil. But here she was, confiding the secrets of her heart.

Sara balled up her trash and stood up. "Sorry, I've got to get back. Maybe I'll see you later."

Andy went with her. It was almost her turn at a booth soon, too. That left me, Phil, and Rebecca.

Rebecca was trying to be cool about it, but the truth was, she couldn't stop looking for Scott. Her head tracked sort of like a satellite dish. She suddenly popped up out of her seat.

"Think I'll get another water. Be right back. Anyone want anything?"

"No thanks," I said with a smile.

"I'm good," Philomena chimed in.

"You are hereby requested to guard this with your life," Becca said, putting the bear on the table beside me.

"Sure," I said. "No problem."

I watched her walk over to the cold drink line. Sure enough, Scott was standing a few customers ahead and Lindsay was nowhere in sight. Good thinking, Rebecca.

Phil finished up the last bite of her pizza. "So, aside from the pie in the face, how are things going with Jackson?"

"All right."

"So, he still makes you feel . . . happy?"

I thought of the shaving cream kiss. "Yeah. He does."

Phil gave me one of her patented, long, searching looks—the kind that make me acutely conscious of every word I said. Yes, I had just told her the truth. But only part of it.

And yet, I couldn't just admit that she had been right. Sure, Jackson had his problems, but I was helping him. We talked about it. He had promised me that he wouldn't steal again. End of story.

Philomena took a sip of her water and looked at me. She wasn't doing anything unusual, but all of a sudden I felt this strange tingling at the back of my neck, slipping down my spine. Like a slow current of electricity. As if I was literally connecting with something.

She knows I am not telling her something, I thought.

"It's hard, isn't it?" she asked. "To know what to do to help someone? Even when you think you know what's right. When you think you know right from wrong."

"I do know right from wrong," I said.

The tingling along my spine got a little stronger.

"I'm not really supposed to do this," Philomena went on.

"Do what?"

"Give advice. Specific instruction. But . . . sometimes it's important to step back, to give yourself emotional distance so you can see clearly."

"I'm seeing perfectly clearly," I said. "Jackson and I are honest with each other. We talk things through."

"That may not be enough," Philomena said.

This time I was staring at her. "Okay, I admit Jackson might need some help. But I am helping him. What more do you expect?"

Philomena's thin shoulders lifted in a shrug. "Well, maybe you're not the one who should act on what you know. Not this time."

I thought my brain was going to explode. "Why is it," I asked, "that I never know what you're talking about? Could you please be a little more specific? I should help. But then not help. It's Jackson. It isn't Jackson. What?"

Philomena didn't respond to my anger. She never does. "When we help people . . . we aren't instigators. I guess you could say we're more like guides. Sometimes, the people we're supposed to be there for aren't even aware of us at all. The more you make it about you, the less you help."

I sat still, trying to absorb her words. Fall fair could have been a thousand miles away.

"Then what's the point?"

"I think you know the answer to that one," Philomena said. Which was just another way of saying that she was reverting to true form: being completely oblique. Her brief and unexpected burst of straight talk was over.

Rebecca returned with her bottle of water. She sat down across from me, beaming.

"How was the cold drink line?"

"Great!" She leaned over, including Phil in the private discussion. "Scott asked me for my screen name. He said he's going to IM me tonight!"

"Late-breaking news," I teased. "Big developments in our top story . . ."

I was happy things seemed to be working out for Rebecca. I had never really seen her go after a guy like this before. It was clear Scott Hammond was really important to her.

"That's great, Rebecca," Philomena chimed in. "I hope everything turns out the way you want it to." She stood up and picked up her trash. "I've got to go. See you guys."

"There, you see?" Rebecca said as soon as Philomena was out of ear shot. "That's just exactly what I mean."

"What's exactly like what you mean?"

"That last comment Philomena made—about how she hoped everything turns out the way I want it to. As if it won't. And I'm being stupid for hoping."

"I don't think that's what she meant," I said carefully. "Phil is weird but kind of literal. She probably meant exactly what she said."

Rebecca shook her head. "She thinks I'm nuts for thinking Scott might really like me. She doesn't think I have a chance against someone like Lindsay."

"I'm sure that's not true," I said, wondering how I got put in the position of defending Philomena, someone *I* barely understood. "Believe me, Phil isn't very impressed by Lindsay Wexler."

Rebecca thought about that for a moment then said, "Maybe I *should* just take things a little more slowly. Not pin all my hopes and dreams on Scott IMing me."

"Could be." Philomena had planted a seed, I realized, leaving Rebecca to do the rest.

The whole guide thing.

All of a sudden, I felt that same tingle I had earlier, stronger than ever, even though Philomena was nowhere around. Connections; maybe I was starting to make them.

"Come on," Rebecca said suddenly, snapping me out of my reverie. She shot to her feet. "Let's see where she goes. Let's follow her."

"Wait a minute," I said, unable to keep up with her lightning-quick changes of mind. "We just got here."

"What difference does that make?" Rebecca asked.

"I want to know more about Philomena. Who she really is. I have a car. Our parents don't expect us to be home for hours. It's the perfect chance."

"Becca," I began, "it is flat-out creepy to spy on your friends. I don't want to be a spy."

"We're not spying," Rebecca argued. "Listen, Philomena is different from anyone I've ever met. Sometimes she makes me uncomfortable. Other times she makes me feel like . . . I don't know, like, some angel is smiling down on me. I just want to know who she is." Becca took a breath. "And you can't tell me, can you?"

I shook my head. I wanted to know, too. I'd been curious ever since Philomena first walked into my life. But now that we were supposedly working together, she was more mysterious than ever. It was driving me crazy.

"I'm going, whether or not you come with me," Becca said quietly.

She set off toward the parking lot.

And I followed.

Philomena's distinctive yellow VW Bug pulled out of the parking lot, just as Rebecca and I got into her car.

Rebecca waited a few minutes, then pulled out, trailing the VW onto Main Street, careful to stay a safe distance behind.

"This is ridiculous," I said. "I feel like we're in a bad cop show."

"What are you so afraid of finding out?" Rebecca asked.

"Nothing," I said. "I would just hate it if any of my friends trailed me."

"But they don't because you give people straight answers," Rebecca said.

Sometimes, I thought.

Ahead of us, Philomena was driving just the way you'd think she would—exactly at the speed limit, always using her turn signals, coming to a full stop at each stop sign. She was like a commercial for safe driving.

I glanced at Rebecca. "What do you think we're going to discover?"

"I don't have the faintest idea," she admitted after a moment.

"Where are we, anyway?" Rebecca suddenly asked.

We had been following Philomena blindly, not really paying all that much attention to where we were going. Now I could see we were all the way across town. On the far side of the city, in a neighborhood I'd never seen before. One that looked like it was struggling.

We followed Philomena to a quiet street where a row of small, narrow houses stood side by side. The narrow alleys in between were barely wide enough to accommodate the cars.

Philomena parked in front of a large white building, farther up the street. We drove past, then Rebecca pulled over and double-parked a few cars down from the Bug.

"What now, Sherlock?" I asked. "How about we just go home—before we totally embarrass ourselves?"

"Will you just wait a minute?" Rebecca snapped. "Watch in the rearview mirror. See where she goes."

I glanced in the mirror in time to see Philomena get out of her car and go inside the building. We were too far away to see if anyone greeted her at the door. Or even what the big building was for. It didn't look like an apartment house, or a store, or even an office.

"Drive around the block," I said. "I want to get a closer look at that building. Maybe we can figure out what it's used for."

Rebecca drove slowly around the block. By the time we got back to the building Philomena had entered, there was a space across the street.

"There—park there," I said, pointing. "I'll get out and peek inside. Then we'll leave."

"Are you crazy?" Rebecca exclaimed. "What if she sees you? She'll think you followed her."

"Well, we did, remember?"

I knew what I was doing was wrong—or at least not terribly nice—but by this time, I was so curious I couldn't stop myself. I opened the door and got out of the car.

The street was bare of trees; the afternoon sunlight a white glare that cast everything it touched in a shimmering outline—the cars, the rooftops. More like midday in July than November.

There wasn't a soul on the street, not like the others we had passed through to get here. No mothers pushing strollers or kids on skateboards. It was quiet in an eerie way.

I walked up to the building, which was square, whitewashed cement, two stories high. No windows on the second floor, just two large doors in the center at the top of a short flight of steps.

It's a church, I thought. Why hadn't I realized that before? Maybe because it was such a strange looking one. Probably an old warehouse or something in a previous life.

I pulled open one of the big front doors and stepped inside. It was cool and dimly lit, mostly by flickering candles. After the glaring sunlight in the street, it took a while for my eyes to adjust.

The sanctuary was a big square room, with wooden pews in two rows on either side of a center aisle. I stood behind the last pew, feeling awkward. I gazed around slowly but didn't see Philomena anywhere.

The church had a simple, open floor plan. There weren't any alcoves or niches where Phil might be hiding. At least I couldn't see any from where I stood.

There was one other person in the church, an older woman kneeling in a pew up front, her head bowed over her hands as she prayed. She wore a shapeless, gray wool coat and had a scarf tied over her head. Her eyes were closed. I wasn't certain, but I thought she might be crying. I couldn't hear anything, but there was something about the way her shoulders moved up and down in a quick, jerky rhythm.

You should just go, Grace, I thought. I knew what it felt like to need to cry but not want anyone to watch.

But a stubborn streak pushed me forward. If there was a side door—a place Philomena might have slipped out—I needed to see it with my own eyes. I walked quietly up the side aisle to the front of the church, sat at the end of a pew, and looked all around.

Nothing. Philomena was nowhere to be seen. Her car was right out front, plain and bright as day. She was nowhere at all.

I looked up at the altar where a simple table stood covered with a white cloth. On top of it rested a beautiful arrangement of flowers. Sunflowers and pink flox, yellow mums and white daisies. Even some white and yellow roses. It looked totally out of place in the stark little church. Like it belonged on a magazine cover.

Staring at the flowers, I noticed a door at the rear of the altar, way in the back and disguised to blend in with the painted wall. I was just trying to get up my courage to go exploring when I heard a gasp behind me.

The old woman had gotten to her feet. I was right. She had been crying. I could still see the streaks the tears had made down her cheeks.

She was staring at the bouquet of flowers as if she had never seen one before.

"Merciful heavens," she whispered in a voice that carried to every inch of the small church. "My prayers have been answered."

And then, as I watched, she began to weep once more. Concern for her won out over my desire to find Philomena.

"Are you all right?" I asked, moving toward her. "Is there something I can do to help you?"

"You've already done it, my dear," the woman said as she wiped the tears from her eyes. They weren't tears of sadness I realized, as I got a little closer. Not anymore. They were tears of joy.

"You brought them, didn't you?" she said, inclining her head toward the flowers. "I don't know how you knew, but I bless you for it."

I hated to disillusion her when she looked so happy. But there was nothing else I could do. I was hardly going to lie standing inside a church.

"I didn't bring them," I said. "They were here when I got here. I'm sorry."

"Don't be," the woman said at once.

She came out from the pew and, before I quite realized what she intended, took me by the arm. She had that smell some old people have, sort of like musty paper. But her grip was strong. Together, we walked until we stood directly in front of the flower arrangement.

"My husband passed away, a year ago tomorrow. There's going to be a special service for him in the morning, but I couldn't afford any flowers. I've been feeling so bad about it. My Harry loved to garden so.

"So I came into the church to pray, and to ask him to forgive me—to understand if I couldn't do what I wanted. That it didn't mean I didn't love him with all my heart.

"Then I looked up, and there were the flowers."

I felt it then, a heat that coursed up my arm and filled my entire body. I'd only had that feeling once before. When Philomena once reached out to comfort me.

Sometimes the people we help don't even know we're there, she had said, not more than an hour ago.

I couldn't see her anywhere. But I could see the flowers.

"You're quite sure you didn't bring them?" the old woman asked. "There's no need to be modest."

"I'm sure," I said. "But I would have, if I'd known."

"Well then," the old woman said, as if my answer satisfied her. She gave my arm a pat. "That's something, isn't it? We'd better go now, my dear. I need to shut off the lights and lock the front door. But I'll know the flowers will be here, waiting for me in the morning."

I nodded. She released my arm, and we walked toward the door.

"I almost forgot to ask," she said, right before I reached it. "You're not a regular member of the congregation, are you? I don't think I remember seeing you before. We don't get many young people these days."

"No," I said. "I'm not."

"Then what made you come in, if you don't mind my asking?"

"I was looking for someone."

The old woman cocked her head. "And I was the only one here," she said. "I'm sorry."

"Don't be," I said. "I'm not. And I hope the service for your husband is everything you hope."

"I'm sure it will be," she answered. "Now."

She gave a wave, and I stepped out the door into the strange white sunshine.

Six

TWO WEEKS INTO MY JOB, there was no way around the truth. I liked it. I liked it a lot.

I even liked all the things I'd started out thinking would be a drag. Learning twenty million new things. Being willing to tell a customer I didn't know the answer to a question, then figuring it out. I didn't even mind the way working at AR cut into my social life.

Though, actually, since Jackson also worked at AR, I suppose you could say that having a job actually improved it. At least on the romance front.

Much as I hated to admit it, my parents had been right. Having a job *was* good for me—not that I had any intention of telling them this, of course.

Since my harvest-themed window had been such a big hit, on Wednesday afternoon Ms. Newberry asked me to set up a display inside the store with an item she had just started carrying—a new brand of whole-grain pasta. She had a few props on hand, but wasn't sure how to arrange them with the boxes and make it all look appetizing.

I worked on it for about an hour, using a big old-fashioned white enamel pot and a china soup bowl and dish set on a little painted wooden table she had in the stockroom.

"Grace . . . that's beautiful!" She walked around the display, checking it from different angles. "I would have never thought to set it up that way. We're going to sell plenty. I better order another case."

She smiled. "I think I'm going to make lavender your official color," she said.

"Whatever floats your boat."

The words were out of my mouth before I could stop. I gave an inward groan. Not precisely the way an employee usually talks to her employer.

Ms. Newberry threw back her head and laughed. "My father used to say that," she told me. "It used to drive my mother absolutely crazy. I think that's half the reason he kept it up."

"My brother used to say it, too," I admitted. "I guess that's why it just sort of slipped out."

"I didn't know you had a brother, Grace," Ms. Newberry said. "Older or younger?"

"Older," I said, surprising myself by answering so readily. "His name was Matt. He died in a car accident this past summer."

Ms. Newberry was silent for a moment, regarding me steadily. "I'm sorry to hear that," she said quietly. "I'm sure that's hard on you."

"It's getting better," I heard myself say.

"It does that," Ms. Newberry said.

For a moment, I thought she was going to say something more. Instead, she gave a brisk little shake of her head as she glanced at her watch.

"Gracious!" she exclaimed. "Is that the time? I had no idea it was so late. I have to get ready to go."

"Big date?" I joked.

To my surprise, Ms. Newberry turned a bright and vivid red. "It's not really a date," she confided. "It's just a meeting with one of the sales reps. We've known each other for years. But he did ask if it could be a dinner meeting."

I was kind of amazed she was telling me all this. It made feel as if she really trusted me, almost like a friend. And it made me want to confide in her.

"I have a date tonight, myself," I said. "With Jackson."

"Jackson," Ms. Newberry said. "From the music department?"

I nodded. "He was my brother's best friend. I've had a crush on him for years. We just started going out."

"How lovely," Ms. Newberry said at once. "I'm so happy for you. I'm sure the fact that he's your brother's friend makes it even more special for you, Grace."

Take that, Philomena, I thought. Here was someone who understood that my complicated relationship with Jackson could be a good thing for him—for both of us.

"Thanks, Ms. Newberry," I said. "I'd just like to say . . . I'm really glad I have this job."

"And I'm glad I hired you, Grace," Ms. Newberry said. She cocked her head to one side, giving me that appraising look.

"Come with me," she said. She set off at a brisk pace toward the clothing and accessories area of the store. "Personally, I think we both need to find a little something red to wear tonight."

"Red. That's for optimism, right?" I asked.

"Absolutely right," Ms. Newberry answered with a smile.

For our first official date, Jackson took me to a Greenwood, Ohio, institution: Sandy's Diner.

This may not sound like a big deal to you. Trust me, it was. In fact, there's sort of a local tradition that says when a couple gets serious, Sandy's is the first place they go.

The fact that no one can quite remember how the tradition started only adds to the mystique. But

Sandy's is also just plain fun. The diner itself is actually an old railroad car. The whole history of it is posted on the wall just inside the front door.

There's a long counter with short stools on one side and a line of booths along the other. Sandy, the owner, still works the grill herself. I have no idea how old she is. I don't think anybody does. She's looked exactly the same for as long as I can remember.

I'd had my suspicions—okay, make that my hopes—about where Jackson and I might be going. But I didn't know for sure until he pulled up in front of the diner.

We got out of the car and walked toward the front door. *Say something, Grace,* I thought. How did you tell a guy you were happy he'd taken you to the one place in town that would show the whole world he was serious about you?

"I haven't been to Sandy's since Matt and I were little," I said, as we went inside. The sign on the cash register said SEAT YOURSELF. Jackson took me by one elbow and steered me toward a booth in the far corner.

"We used to beg our parents to take us here every single time we got in the car."

We slid into the booth, facing each other.

"That must have been the year your dad went on his health kick," Jackson commented. He rested his arms on the table, then extended one toward me, palm up. I slid my hand into his.

This is for real, I thought. *I'm sitting in Sandy's with Jackson Turner, who is now officially my boyfriend!*

"Didn't your father go through one whole summer when he wanted you guys to walk everywhere?" Jackson went on.

"That's it exactly!" I exclaimed, laughing. "I'd forgotten that."

Jackson smiled and rolled his eyes. "I never will," he said. "I think it's all Matt talked about that whole year, how your dad had lost his mind."

Our waitress arrived. She handed us each a menu, several pages accordioned together and covered in thick plastic with a red border. Red is Sandy's signature color.

Red for optimism, I suddenly realized. No wonder so many couples decided to start their relationships here.

I made a mental note to mention this to Ms. Newberry. At her insistence, I was wearing a new pair of earrings, red enamel drops. They were the bright spot, contrast against the soft, clingy sweater in a color the catalogue had described as wild oats and black skinny jeans.

"What was your favorite thing to order when you were a kid?" Jackson asked. He released my hand so he could flip through the menu, but, beneath the table, I felt the way his leg pressed against mine.

"Pigs in a blanket," I said at once. At Sandy's, pigs

in a blanket means pancakes curled around link sausages. You slather them with butter and lots of maple syrup.

I laughed at the memory and Jackson said, "What's so funny?"

"I think I just figured out why my parents used to dread taking us here—probably because Matt and I always came home covered in syrup."

"You weren't supposed to eat the pancakes with your fingers," Jackson said with a mock frown.

"Yeah, but we always did it, anyway."

"Me, too," he confessed with a grin. He shut the menu with a decisive snap. "That's exactly what I'm ordering. Pigs in a blanket. With scrambled eggs on the side."

"But that's what I want!" I protested. "Without the eggs."

"Go for it," Jackson said at once.

The waitress came back with two glasses of ice water, and we placed our orders. Jackson ordered a milk shake to go with his. I ordered a soda. As soon as she was gone, Jackson reached across the table for my hands again.

"It's really great being here with you, Grace," he said. "There's so much stuff in my life that's still going wrong. But this . . ."

He broke off, gazing down at our entwined hands. "This feels good. It feels right."

"I think so, too," I said.

He looked up quickly, his whole face lit up in a smile.

I did that, I thought. Not in a big egotistical sort of way. But it *was* sort of a charge. Not only was I right in the middle of the romance I had dreamed of for years, but being with me made Jackson feel good.

It was helping. *I* was helping. Just by being with him. Philomena had made it sound so complicated, when really it wasn't. All I had to do was to be myself.

"How are things going with the band?" I asked as the waitress delivered our orders.

"Great," Jackson said. He doused his rolled up pancakes in syrup, and I took my first bite of pancake and sausage. *Pure heaven,* I thought.

"We kind of struggled at first, you know? With Matt gone," Jackson said, "we sort of floundered. The chemistry was totally different. We had to figure out who we were, what we wanted to sound like, all over again."

"So things are better now?"

Jackson nodded enthusiastically. "They are. We've been practicing almost every day, getting really tight. And we turned in all the paperwork for the Battle. You wouldn't believe how many rules and regs there are. It's practically like applying for college."

At the mention of college, he let out a sigh. I decided to avoid the topic.

"I've been working on the CD cover," I said. "I think it's almost done."

We discussed what I was doing, what songs the band was thinking of playing in the competition. Some of that depended on how far they got. Sort of like *American Idol*, bands got eliminated as the competition progressed.

Our meal was over almost before I knew it.

"So," Jackson said as the waitress dropped the check on our table. "It's a school night."

I nodded. "I've got to be home by eight-thirty."

"Me, too," he said. "I've got a history test tomorrow. I should probably at least look at my books. But . . . um . . . let's do this again sometime, okay?"

"Definitely," I told him.

After paying for both of us, which made me feel all melted inside, Jackson drove me home. He parked a couple of doors down from the house, which only goes to show he could read my mind. It wasn't that I didn't want my parents to know there had been a change in Jackson's and my relationship. I just didn't want anything to spoil the mood. Like parental questions that required explanations.

I wanted the end of our first real date to be like the rest: just right.

He switched off the engine and pulled me close. I rested my head against his shoulder.

"I had a really great time tonight," I said.

"Me, too," Jackson said quietly. He tipped my face up, gave me a lingering kiss. "I suppose we're sort of official now, huh?"

In the light of the streetlamp, I could see that his eyes were teasing.

"Hey, you're the one who picked Sandy's," I replied.

"Would you believe I've never taken a girl there before?"

"Bet that's what you say to all of us."

"It figures," Jackson said, still teasing. "I should have known Matt would blow my secret."

We fell silent. I could feel his heart beat through the leather of his coat.

"I miss him," Jackson said quietly. "Sometimes, I just miss Matt so much."

"I do, too," I said. "But I think . . ." I paused, wanting to choose my words with care. "I think I'm figuring out how to go on. I'm trying to make my thoughts of him a good thing, a celebration."

I shifted so that I could look up into Jackson's face. "Does that make any sense at all?"

"Yeah," he said softly, and I thought I detected relief in his tone. "Yeah, it does. I didn't know how to put it, but you got it just right."

Again, I felt that surge of positive energy, of hope. Philomena *had* been wrong. My ability to help Jackson through his tough times wasn't compromised by the fact that we were falling for each other. That aspect only made the bonds between us stronger.

"I'd better go in," I said. "It *is* a school night."

"Okay," he sighed. "I'll IM you later, okay?"

"Okay," I said.

We had a long, slow kiss good night. Then I slid out of the car and walked toward my house. Just as I reached the front walk, Jackson drove by with a quick toot of his horn.

I watched until his car had turned the corner, then walked up to the front door.

Maybe it was just my imagination, but all the way up the walk, I had this image of Matt's face. Looking down from wherever he was. And smiling.

Rebecca seemed to have given up on solving "The Mystery of Philomena." She hadn't mentioned it since that day we followed Phil. I never told her what I saw in the church, about the flowers.

Still, I kept thinking about that woman grieving for her husband. I was sure that like me, she was one of the people Philomena had been sent to help. I had no doubt that the flowers came from Philomena. What I wondered about, though, was whether

I had been *meant* to see them. Maybe it wasn't just Rebecca's paranoia—and my own frustration with Phil—that led me into that church. Maybe I was meant to see that old woman's sorrow transformed into joy—some sort of cosmic lesson about what helping someone really looks like.

I hadn't tried to ask Philomena about it; it would have been too embarrassing to admit that we followed her that day. Actually, I was trying to keep my interactions with Phil as normal as possible. Which meant they were mostly limited to seeing each other at lunch.

After the school fair, Philomena became a regular at our lunch table. She no longer asked if she could sit with us. She was just there. Andy and Sara were fine with it; they were starting to accept Phil, maybe even like her. Even Rebecca no longer seemed weirded out by her, but that was probably because Rebecca was nearly obsessed with thoughts of Scott Hammond.

The day after my "official" first date with Jackson, I sat down at our table, dying to tell everyone the news. Rebecca, however, was already off on another riff about Scott.

". . . so he couldn't call back until around ten, because my brother wouldn't get off the computer any earlier." Rebecca rolled her eyes. "Talk about a techno hog. So when he finally did call . . ." She leaned forward and dropped her voice. "He asked me if I wanted to go to the movies on Saturday night!"

I laughed as Sara and Andy instantly began to applaud.

"Oh, no, you guys. Cool it," Rebecca begged. But a blind person could have seen how pleased and excited she was. She unwrapped her sandwich, grinning from ear to ear.

"So . . . you're going, right?" I asked.

She stared at me as if I'd grown an extra head.

"What do you think? Of course I'm going."

We all laughed, even Philomena.

"The only surprise is that it took him so long to ask you out," Andy commented.

"I think," Rebecca said thoughtfully, and I saw her shoot a quick glance in Phil's direction, "that Scott is actually a little shy. He covers it up with a certain amount of jock behavior. Not that he's obnoxious or anything," she added quickly.

"Of course not," Philomena said. "You wouldn't be interested in him if he was." She smiled at Rebecca, and I could almost see Becca relax. "He's nice."

"He *is* nice. Very nice." Rebecca was almost glowing with happiness, as if she had just won that stuffed bear all over again.

"I guess this means Lindsay Wexler is out of the picture," I said.

Rebecca shrugged and took a bite of a very juicy apple. "We'll see. That kind of girl never gives up."

"Don't worry about her," Andy advised. "One thing about Lindsay, she has a short attention span. Now that she knows Scott really isn't interested, she'll zero in on some other guy." She gathered up her books. "I have an appointment with my guidance counselor. I'd better go."

"Me, too." Sara stood up and gulped down the rest of her juice. "I have to return a library book before the fine gets any higher. I already owe a dollar-fifty."

Rebecca looked at the clock on the wall and groaned. "And I have a lacrosse team meeting. Later," she said, heading out of the cafeteria at a run.

That left me and Philomena at the table. The rest of the kids in the cafeteria were talking and laughing and making all kinds of noise. But it felt as if a bubble of silence had fallen over us.

Philomena was eating her sandwich and glanced up at me. "How is your sketch for the CD cover coming? I liked what you showed me in study hall."

"It's okay," I said. "I told Jackson about the idea, and he liked it, so I'm working up something he can show to the rest of the band."

"So things are going well with Jackson?"

"They're going great," I said. "We went to Sandy's Diner last night." I suddenly realized Philomena would have no idea of what a date at Sandy's signified.

She nodded, and said, "I hear they have good food."

"Yeah," I agreed, "they do."

I wondered if I should tell her that we were officially going out. Or that I had already helped Jackson. I didn't say any of it, partly because I didn't want to get into it if she didn't approve. And partly because I figured she knew everything, anyway.

"I like your friends, Grace," Philomena said suddenly, taking me totally by surprise. "Not only are they nice individually, you're good together as a group. You really support one another, balance each other out."

"We do, don't we?" Of course I knew this already. It was why we had all stayed friends for so long. But it felt different somehow to have Philomena say it, right out loud.

She had also said that she and I would be working together to help others. So far I hadn't noticed any great teamwork between us. Okay, I had decided to help Jackson on my own, but still, I kept expecting her to come up with some big, important mission for the two of us—save a puppy from a tornado or something. Of course, I wasn't sure how to bring this up.

"My friends and I, we help each other out," I said.

"Yes, I know you do."

"Does that count?" I asked. "That kind of helping, I mean."

"You sound as if you're keeping score." She gave me one of her smiles, the kind that said she loved me, even when I was making no sense at all. "I'm not sure what you're getting at," she went on. "All I can tell you is that it all matters, good and bad, everything we do."

The bell rang, signaling the end of lunch period. I got up, sliding my books into the crook of one arm.

"Grace," Philomena said as she got to her feet. "I think Jackson is a good person. He means well, and I know he loved Matt. So I understand your feelings about him."

No, you don't, I thought.

"Jackson is under a lot of pressure, Grace."

"And he's dealing with his problems," I told her. "He—" I didn't want to rat on Jackson. "He made some mistakes but he's on the right track now."

"I suppose that's possible," Philomena said. "But you know how easy it is to fall off the right track. So . . . just keep your eyes open, okay?"

"They are open," I said.

"Are they?" she asked gently. Then she picked up her books and walked off.

"How are you coming with the cartoons for the year-book, Grace? Any progress?" Ms. Kaplanski asked later that afternoon when English class was over.

I felt a pang of guilt at her words. I hadn't totally neglected my yearbook assignment. I had been doodling around a bit. But the sketches were still pretty rough, and I didn't have nearly enough of them.

"I've made a good start," I said, trying to put a positive spin on things. "But a little more time would be great. How soon were you hoping for them?"

Ms. Kaplanski considered a moment. "We're still planning out the different sections of the book at this point. You have some time. But I showed the art editor the sketches you turned in last week. I can tell you right now she's definitely going to want more, and so do I."

A quick surge of pleasure replaced the guilt. No two ways about it; it was nice to be wanted.

"I'm glad those sketches are okay. I'll try to work faster," I promised.

"There's a yearbook meeting Friday afternoon," Ms. Kaplanski went on. "Maybe you should come and hear all this firsthand. It might make things easier for you."

And easier for Ms. Kaplanski, too, I thought. She was a good sport to keep after me like this, trying to keep me involved. A lot of other teachers would have given up.

"I have to work at Alternate Realities on Friday," I said.

"Oh, that's right." Ms. Kaplanski brightened. "I think Rebecca mentioned you had an after-school job. Congratulations. I hope you like it."

"Thanks. I do," I said. "Maybe I could come to the next yearbook meeting—if it wasn't on a Friday?"

Ms. Kaplanski smiled. "I think that would be great, Grace," she said. "I'll see what I can do to help with scheduling, then keep you posted. Keep working on those cartoons. Without them, the book will be awfully dull."

I nodded and smiled at her. "I'll do what I can."

Make that *definitely* nice to be wanted.

I had the afternoon off from Alternate Realities. When I got home, I had the house to myself. Both my parents were at work and wouldn't be home for a few hours.

It was hard being home alone—without Matt.

Too many silences, holes that could never be filled. I went into the kitchen, set my backpack down on the table, and opened the fridge in search of a snack. And there they were, a whole line of them in the bottom shelf of the door.

Beer bottles.

Only a couple of months ago, this was the time

of day when I'd done my best drinking. Sitting quietly in the kitchen doing my homework, letting the cool slide of alcohol down my throat distract me from the silent emptiness of the house around me.

Wiley padded into the kitchen. I patted his smooth head and gave him a dog biscuit.

Then I opened the fridge again. I picked up one of the chilled green bottles. *One beer,* I thought. One beer wouldn't hurt. And it would take the edge off, the edge of loneliness.

I opened the bottle and took three quick swigs. It tasted good—cold and slightly bitter but somehow refreshing. I hadn't eaten anything since lunch, so the buzz hit almost at once. Something inside me relaxed, and that lonely edge didn't feel quite so sharp anymore.

I set the bottle on the table and took my books out of my pack, ready to start my homework. It was just like easing into my old routine.

Which nearly killed you.

I stiffened, not sure where that thought came from—a message from Philomena? Matt? My own slightly messed-up self?

In any case, I knew it was the truth. I poured the rest of the bottle into the kitchen sink, and for a long moment just sat there, realizing how little it took to slip back into my old habits, how easy it was to fall off the right track.

I winced as I thought of my last conversation with Philomena. I had just very neatly proved her point.

I'm not going to drink, I promised myself. *That's over now.* But I couldn't help wishing that the thing that led me to drink in the first place—the pain over Matt's death—was over, too.

All of a sudden, I made a decision. I hadn't gone into Matt's room more than a handful of times since he died. It was just too hard. My mom hadn't been able to bring herself to change a thing. The room looked exactly the way it always had, every single day that Matt was alive.

But today, I wanted to be near him. I wanted to feel his things around me. Maybe those traces of Matt could be a comfort instead of proof of his loss. I had told Ms. Newberry that things were getting better. And they were. I was with Jackson now.

Jackson. When I was with Jackson, that lonely edge just melted away.

I climbed the stairs to Matt's room and slowly pushed the door open. I stood in the doorway and took a long deep breath. The shades were drawn to inches above the windowsill, and dust motes floated in a shaft of fading sunlight. My mother came in once a week to dust and vacuum. Otherwise she kept the door closed, and left the room alone.

How long before my parents decided to put

Matt's things away? I wondered. To turn the room that had been his into a spare bedroom or a TV room? To acknowledge, once and for all, that Matt was never coming home?

It had been four months since the accident.

How did you decide what was enough time?

I walked into his room, moved slowly around it, looking at all of Matt's things. Books, sports trophies, geodes, and old banks still full of coins. The longer I stayed, the more I felt like he was somewhere nearby. Like he might walk into the room any minute and get mad at me for messing around with his stuff or borrowing something without asking.

Like, if I listened long and hard enough, I might actually hear the sound of his voice.

I'd like that, I thought. *I'd like to hear Matt's voice again. Just once.*

I sat down on the bed, feeling the way it dipped beneath my weight. Matt had always liked his mattress sort of dumpy and soft. If I put my back against the wall and stared straight ahead, I could see Matt's bulletin board on the opposite wall.

It was covered with pictures of him and Jackson, and the other guys in the band, too, of course. But most were just of him and Jackson together, a sort of photo montage of their friendship. There was one in particular I noticed right off. The two of them and

Wiley, on that fateful camping trip where they encountered the skunk. Jackson had the same picture pinned to his bulletin board.

I got off the bed, crossed the room, and after a moment's hesitation, took the photo down. Then I walked out of the room and quietly shut the door behind me.

I was just going back to my own room when I heard the phone ring. I checked the number on caller ID.

Turner, Henry, the ID said. That was Jackson's dad's name. The phone must still be in his name, even though he had moved to Chicago.

"Hey, Grace. It's Jackson," I heard his voice come over the machine. "I know it's your day off, and I was thinking you might be home."

"I'm here. I'm here," I said quickly as I punched the button to turn the answering machine off. "Sorry, it took me a minute to pick up."

"Hi," Jackson said, and I thought I heard both hope and uncertainty in his voice. "So, listen, I'm having this thought. I was going through some of our old recordings and I found this cut I thought you might like. Matt's singing on it. I thought you might like, you know . . ."

To hear his voice, I thought.

If this wasn't a Philomena moment, I didn't know what was. I had wished for the sound of Matt's voice, and now it looked as if my wish was going to come true. From an entirely unexpected source.

"You have a cut with Matt on it?" I echoed.

"I do," Jackson said, and I could hear the happiness in his voice. "I was just going through some old tapes of ours, and there it was. I thought maybe you would like to hear it."

"I would," I said, even though all the muscles in my chest got tight at the idea.

My thoughts were spinning. How would it feel to actually hear my brother's voice again? How had it made Jackson feel?

"You work tomorrow, right?" Jackson asked.

"Yeah," I acknowledged. "Maybe after I get off? I think I can clear it with my folks."

"That sounds good."

"I'll see you tomorrow after work, okay?"

"Okay," I said. "And I . . . thanks for the call. Say hi to Sam for me."

"Will do," he said. Slowly, I hung up the phone, then I lifted up my eyes. As if I was staring straight up into the heavens.

"Thank you," I said. Right out loud. If my parents had seen me, they probably would have dialed 911.

But I knew what had happened, or I thought I did. In some strange way, a way I never could have predicted, I had Matt back.

He'd come home.

Seven

"HEY, GRACE. COME ON IN." Jackson answered the door at my first knock. I followed him inside.

"I set up the tape in my dad's old study. Better speakers than the ones in my room."

"Okay. Sure." I was glad Jackson wasn't making small talk, that we were going to get right to it.

I trailed him down the hall, feeling both excited and a little scared.

"You want a soda or something?"

"No, thanks. I'm good."

He opened the study door. The room was still the weird combination of adult furniture covered by teenage stuff.

"Pick your spot," Jackson said. "I'll just go get everything cued up."

I headed for the far end of the couch while he went over to the stereo system and fiddled around with the controls. From where I was sitting, I could see the bulletin board he had put up. There was the picture of the camping trip. The same one I had taken from Matt's room, the one that was now pinned to the center of my own bulletin board. Arranged so that I could see the two of them together from pretty much any position in my room—particularly first thing when I opened my eyes in the morning.

All of a sudden, I swallowed a lump in my throat.

"Okay," Jackson said as he hooked up his laptop to the speakers in his dad's office. "I think I've got it lined up right. Here it is. Here's the cut."

I heard the *click* as he pressed the on-screen play button. Then, quickly, he moved to the couch. He sat in the middle, not close enough to touch me, as if sensing I might need space.

The music started slowly; I recognized one of Matt's trademark guitar riffs, and then Jackson playing bass in the background. Then Matt started singing. It was a slow tune, sort of a ballad. But not syrupy or sentimental. The lyrics were sharp and smart.

Original. Just like Matt himself.

It was so strange to hear his voice again, even though it was what I'd wanted. I closed my eyes, pretending for a moment that Matt was just in another room, his bedroom maybe, fooling around on the guitar while I was in my room, trying to study or on the computer.

I'd bang on the wall when he got too loud.

I leaned back, my head against the sofa cushion, savoring the sound. It brought back so many images. So many memories. It helped me see Matt clearly in my mind's eye. He was vivid. Alive.

The song was coming to an end and I felt my eyes fill up with tears. I wasn't even sure what kind. Sadness and happiness so mixed together I couldn't separate them even if I tried.

I took a shaky breath, and heard Jackson shift on the couch. I opened my eyes. He was looking at me, his expression serious. I thought his eyes looked a little glassy, too. But before I could be sure, the song ended. There was just some blank space, an odd, empty sound of nothingness.

Jackson got up and stopped the tape player. Then he just stood for a moment without turning around.

"I remember that song," I said. "I didn't know he'd finished it."

"I don't know that it really *was* finished," Jackson replied. "We just turned the recorder on one afternoon when we were fooling around."

He rubbed his eyes with the back of his hand. "There's just one spot, in the last chorus, that sounds so lame. Matt could never hit that high note."

I laughed. "Yeah, I know. He always wanted to hit it, thought it would sound cool, but he couldn't quite pull it off."

Jackson turned to me with a smile. It felt good

to share these feelings with someone who knew my brother almost as well as I did. In some ways, Jackson knew him even better. He probably knew things about Matt I would never know.

Secrets, I thought. We all have them. Some dark, some not.

Jackson took a disk out of the machine and handed it to me. "Here, I made this one for you. I have another copy."

"Thanks," I said. "That's really nice."

We looked at each other for a moment, as if now that we no longer had Matt to share, neither of us knew quite what to say. Hearing Matt's voice again was a big deal for both of us.

"I thought the sound quality was pretty good," Jackson said at last. "My father went for the best when he bought this equipment. I'm surprised he didn't take the whole system with him to Chicago."

His face twisted in an attempt at a smile that didn't quite get there. "I guess he couldn't figure out how to pack it up quickly. He did make a pretty fast getaway."

"Do you hear from him at all?" I asked.

He shrugged and sat on the couch again. "Once in a while. Whenever it's convenient for him, as far as I can tell. He's off in his own world now. It doesn't matter."

"Of course it matters," I said. "What he's doing

hurts you, and it hurts Sam. If I were you, I'd be so furious—"

"You got that right," he said.

"Do you know when the divorce will be final?" I asked. I was sort of feeling my way along. But it seemed to make him feel better to talk about what was happening.

He shook his head. "I don't even know if they've filed the papers yet. My mom talks to her lawyer more than she talks to me."

He was reaching for a "you-think-I-care?" tone. But I knew he felt just the opposite.

"What about your college applications? Did you finish those?"

"I'm still working on my essay. I'm applying for a scholarship at my first-choice school. That's what my guidance counselor said to do. I need letters of recommendation, good ones. I don't know who to ask."

He sounded stressed and stumped. I felt bad for him, dealing with all this on his own. When it came time for me to apply to colleges, I knew it would be a real family project. Last spring, when Matt was only a junior, my father had already picked out a short list of teachers, coaches, and other adults Matt could ask for recommendations. I tried to remember, thinking some of those people might be able to help Jackson, too.

"How about asking Pastor James?" I said. Pastor James was the minister at the church where both our families went. "He knows you really well from the youth group, and I know he likes the band."

"That's a good idea." Jackson sounded surprised at the suggestion. "Pastor James. Why didn't I think of that?"

"Maybe you have one or two other little things on your mind?"

I was thinking about the divorce, but all of a sudden I realized my words could have a second meaning. It sounded like I was fishing for a compliment or for something romantic. I flushed.

Quickly, I slipped the disc into my pack. "Thanks again for this. It really means a lot to me, and I know it will to my parents, too."

"Happy to do it," Jackson said.

"I brought something for you, too," I went on. I reached into the backpack again, brought out an over-sized envelope. "It's just, I guess you'd call it a rough draft at this point. But I thought maybe you could show it to the other guys, see how they like it."

I pulled out the artwork for the CD cover I had been working on. There was the car Charlie had wanted, a sort of cool '50s convertible. Top down, naturally. I had drawn it in candy-apple-red crayon.

The bodies of the band members were this sort

of collage, made from images I cut out from magazines. Charlie was driving the car. He had on an oversized checked jacket with a bright blue tie. Malcolm, the drummer, sat in the passenger seat. Jackson had the backseat all to himself.

I had Photoshopped in black-and-white photos of their heads. Above the car, in a picture-perfect blue sky, floated a series of white clouds that spelled out JOY RIDE.

Jackson didn't say a word. He just stood there, studying it.

"It's okay if you don't like it," I said nervously. "I can make changes."

"No way," he finally said. He looked up with a smile. "It's outstanding, Grace. Exactly what I wanted." He gave a sudden laugh. "Even though I didn't know what that was ahead of time. So many bands wind up with this tired look—like, they're ripping off some famous album and hoping no one will notice. This is just the opposite. It's—I don't know—fresh."

He rolled his eyes, and grinned. "Listen to me. I sound like Mr. Hellesen."

Mr. Hellesen was the drama teacher. He also taught a movie-appreciation course. He was always using words like *fresh* and *edgy* to describe things.

"I just wish—" Jackson began, then broke off.

"The only thing I'd change is that I wish Matt could be in it, somehow."

I felt my heart do a long, slow roll.

"I thought about that," I admitted. "But I didn't know quite know how to work him in, and I thought maybe we should talk about it ahead of time."

"I'll talk to Charlie and Malcolm," Jackson said. "But I know they'll feel the same way."

Spontaneously, he threw his arms around me, lifted me from my feet, and twirled me around. I gave a laugh of pure joy. Jackson Turner was turning out to be full of surprises.

I liked that. I liked it a lot.

"This is going to be so great, Grace," he said as he set me down. He kept his arms around me. "I have a really good feeling about this whole Battle of the Bands. Things are going to start turning around."

"I hope so," I said. "You guys are totally awesome."

Jackson dropped a quick kiss on my lips. "Spoken like a true fan."

I heard the front door slam.

Instantly, Jackson's expression changed. He didn't look so happy and confident now. Instead, I could almost see him pull into himself.

"That's my mom," he said in a low voice.

"Okay," I said. I stepped back out of his arms. "I'll

take that as my cue to go. The guys are coming over to practice anyway, right?"

"Right," Jackson nodded. We walked to the door, opened it, and stepped out into the hall. We almost ran right into his mother.

"Oh, Jackson," Mrs. Turner exclaimed, her whole demeanor sort of harried and distracted. "There you are. Where's Sam?"

Her tone was almost accusatory.

"He's over at Tyler's house." Jackson's voice had gone stiff. "He asked you yesterday if he could go."

Mrs. Turner gave a sigh. "That's right. He did, didn't he?" All of a sudden, she seemed to notice me for the first time. "Hello, Grace," she said. "Have you been here all this time?"

"Just a couple of minutes," I answered. "I brought over some artwork I've been working on. It's for the band's CD cover."

"I see." Mrs. Turner ran a hand through her short hair. "Don't take this the wrong way, Grace, but I think it would be better if you and Jackson weren't alone together in the house. We've had more than enough excitement around here. We don't need anything else to happen."

"Mom," Jackson said sharply.

"Jackson, I'm the one who's responsible for this family now," Mrs. Turner said, her tone exasperated and cross. "You know I can't be watching you and your brother every minute. I have to set some rules."

"I was just going, anyway," I said, giving Jackson's hand a quick squeeze. "I have homework, and I know the rest of the band is coming over. Nice to see you, Mrs. Turner."

I stepped past Jackson, and started down the hall.

"Nice to see you, too, Grace," Mrs. Turner called after me. "Say hi to your folks."

"I'll do that," I said.

"Grace," Jackson called. "Wait up."

"I'm sorry about all that," he said, as we stepped out onto the front porch. "Now you know what it feels like to live around here on a daily basis."

"Don't worry about it." I turned toward him, put my hands on his shoulders. "You just keep focusing on the good stuff," I said. "Everything will turn out all right. Parents always worry about all the wrong things, anyway."

"I am focusing on the good stuff," Jackson said. "In fact, I'm about to get a little more focused right now." As his lips met mine, they curved in a smile.

That night, I had just shut off my light and was lying in bed, about to put on the headphones to my CD player, when my mother came into my room. She had been out at a meeting at church, and I hadn't even heard her come in. She sat on the edge of my bed and looked down at me.

"Hey, Mom. What's up?"

She smoothed out the covers with her hand.

"Does something have to be up?" she asked. "I just wanted to say good night. Some days I feel like I hardly see you. You're at school or at your job. I'm at work and in meetings. We're all so busy around here."

It was true, I thought. When she wasn't working, my mom was at church a lot, doing volunteer work. That was hard for me right after Matt died. She was out all the time, helping other people, leaving me to cope on my own.

But now that I had a little more perspective, I could see that my mom had never realized that part. She had been fighting to keep her head above water, just like me and my dad. Dad had hid out in his basement workshop, distracting himself with one project after another. I had acted out. Each in our own ways, we had been grasping for something to help get us through the pain.

"So, what's going on with you?" she asked now. "Everything okay?"

"Sure." Was she worried about something specific, or was this just a general check-in?

I wish my parents could learn to trust me again, I thought.

"School, friends, everything's good?"

"Everything's fine, Mom. I'm doing some caricatures for Ms. Kaplanski and the yearbook." I knew my mom totally loved it that I worked on the yearbook.

"My friends are all good. Rebecca has a date this weekend with a guy she really, really likes. She's totally psyched."

My mother laughed. "How about you? Who do you like?"

So that's what this is all about, I thought.

"I saw you with Jackson the other night," my mom went on before I could reply. "And I know he's been walking you home a lot.

"I just wanted to say . . . if you like him, Grace, you don't have to worry about me and your father . . . that we might be . . . uncomfortable if you brought Jackson around—"

"Thanks, Mom," I said, knowing that hadn't been easy for her. "I appreciate it."

"I want you to feel you can be honest with us," she went on. "We've all been through a lot. We've all made mistakes, but you don't have to hide things from us or protect us from things going on in your life.

"Even if it's something you think your father and I won't like, we would rather know the truth. And we would rather hear it from you than from anyone else."

"I do like Jackson," I said. "I always have. He's a great guy, and he likes me, too, but it's a little complicated."

"Yes," my mother said. "I know. So much in life is timing, isn't it Grace? Meeting the right person, finding the right job. The important thing, I think, is to stay open to possibilities." She made a face. "I'm trying to learn that lesson myself."

"I love you, Mom," I suddenly said. I leaned over and threw my arms around her. She put hers around me and held on tight.

"I love you, too, Gracie-pie. I love you to the stars."

That's what she always said to me when I was little and she tucked me in. I love you to the stars.

Now I pictured Matt up there, one of those stars, looking down on us tonight.

"'Night, Mom," I said.

My mother gave me one last squeeze, and then let go.

After she left, I lay very still for a long time, staring at the ceiling.

Something's different, I thought. *I'm different. I'm coming to terms with things.*

Like my life.

I knew I could never have Matt back again. But I was coming to understand that wasn't quite the same thing as saying he was gone. We were still connected. Me. Jackson. My parents. Everyone who knew him.

Before, those connections had made me feel sad and frightened. Not tonight. Tonight, they gave me comfort, made me feel strong.

Eight

I MET UP WITH MY FRIENDS on Friday morning before the first bell. They were hanging out in the hallway by Sara's locker. Everyone except Rebecca, who was in the school lobby, talking to Scott.

She walked up to us—or should I say floated?—with that same dreamy look she had been wearing all week.

"We were just figuring out tomorrow night—which movie we should see," she explained.

"So which one is it?" Sara asked.

"More importantly," I said, "what are you going to wear?"

Rebecca looked perplexed. "I'm not sure. I have this black jersey, and my new jeans—"

"The jersey that says number 53 on the back?" I asked.

I love Becca, but her taste in clothing tends toward athletic supply stores. *Time for a wardrobe inter-*

vention, I thought. The question was, how to be dip-lomatic about it.

"That would be okay," I said. "But, you know, I just might have the perfect top for you. That wrap-around sweater I just got at Iridescence? The color would be great on you. Want to borrow it?"

"That top is totally hot," Sara chimed in. We exchanged a quick look. "Grace is right. That deep green would be a great color for you."

"But Grace is so much smaller than I am," Becca pointed out. "What if it's too tight on me?"

Rebecca is definitely bigger than me on top. But not in a bad way, believe me.

"I don't think it would be too tight," Andy spoke up. "That's the beauty of the wraparound style." She rolled her eyes. "Listen to me. I sound just like a saleswoman."

"I don't know." Rebecca looked hesitant.

"I am just about to be brilliant," I said. "How about a spa night at my house? An evening of relax-ation and beauty. We can all bring our favorite out-fits. If you want to, Becca, you can try on every item of clothing in my closet."

"Oh, that sounds perfect," Andy exclaimed at once. "We haven't done that in ages. Say, yes, Becca. It'll be so much fun. Particularly for those of us who are date-challenged. We can live vicariously through you."

When Sara gets excited about an idea, she waves her hands in the air, like she's about to take off. "I know, I know," she said. "My mom just got this foot spa. It vibrates and has little water jets. I'll bring it. It's totally awesome."

"And I found some online recipes for facials," Andy put in. "With oatmeal and avocados and stuff. I can bring all the ingredients."

"Okay, okay," Rebecca put her hands up like the victim of a holdup. "You guys have talked me into it. I'll bring an open mind and myself."

"Perfect!" I said. "I can hardly wait. This is going to be so much fun."

"I've never been to a spa night," Philomena said.

I must have jumped about a mile. She had been so quiet, I hadn't realized she was there.

A stiff little smile was fixed on her face. I could see she wasn't sure if she was included or not. She hadn't actually been part of the group when we started the discussion.

It was my call.

"Sounds like tonight is your chance, then," I said. "You can have the same assignment as Rebecca: Just bring yourself."

Philomena gave me that smile that made every atom in my body feel brighter somehow.

"Thanks, Grace," she said. "Spa night sounds great. I'd love to come."

Late that afternoon, I hurried home from work, arriving just in time to straighten up my room before Spa Night. That was the deal I cut with my mother when I'd phoned her at lunchtime. Clean room, both before and after. Clean kitchen by the end of the night.

She and Dad were going out tonight. But she didn't mind me having my friends over. She even left us money for pizza. She peeked in the doorway, still fastening on one earring, just as I was finishing up. I had pulled a variety of tops out of my drawer and stacked them neatly on the bed.

"Whoa," my mom said as she glanced in through my open bedroom door. "Houston, we have a problem. What's that blue stuff on the floor?"

"That would be the rug, Mom," I said.

Her eyebrows rose. "Well, so it is," she said. "It's been so long since I've seen it, I forgot what color it was."

"Ha ha," I said. "Very funny."

She smiled, enjoying her own joke.

"I picked up some sodas to go with the pizza," she told me. "It's so expensive if you order them with takeout. They're in the fridge getting cold. And I got some ice cream, too."

"Chocolate chip cookie dough?" I asked.

My mother's brow wrinkled, as if she was genuinely perplexed. "Is there any other kind? Just remember not to leave a huge mess in the kitchen, okay? And try to resist the temptation to try on any of my clothes."

"I think we can handle that part, Mom," I said.

She laughed and kissed me on the cheek. "Okay, honey, have fun. Call my cell if you need anything."

My parents had only been gone a few minutes before the doorbell rang. My buds piled into the house all at once. Andy and Sara had gotten a ride with Rebecca, who had her mother's car again, and Philomena drove up at the same time in her yellow Bug.

"I got the stuff for the facials," Andy said, her voice enthusiastic as she made her way to the kitchen. She plunked a brown shopping bag down on the countertop and began to unload it. "The vegetables are all organic."

Sara rolled her eyes. "Of course they are."

Andy stuck her tongue out at her.

I picked up an avocado. "Did you bring any chips to go with this?"

Andy snatched back the avocado. "Hands off. Make yourself useful. Order the pizza."

Andy pulled out her recipes and grabbed an apron. With Philomena and Sara assisting on the chopping and measuring, they started mixing up different concoctions. I headed for the phone. A quick call later, our standard veggie special was on its way. By the time I finished the call, Andy had her first batch of gunk mixed up.

"This looks just like the smoothies they make at AR," I said, giving it a sniff. My eyes widened. "Wow. I don't know if this will clear up my skin, but it's sure doing wonders for my sinuses."

"Let me have some," Rebecca spoke up. She took the bowl from me and began to dab it on her face. Then, before I knew quite what she intended, she reached out with a sticky finger and made a big streak right down my nose.

"Hey!" I said.

"Nice look," Sara commented. She was busy with the second bowl Andy had mixed up. "I like this one—the oatmeal one. It exfoliates, you know."

"Is that good?" Philomena spoke up for the first time. Phil had a unique approach to the facials. She had taken a little bit from each of the bowls. Her face was four different colors.

Sara looked over and laughed. "That's a good idea. I'm going to do some of each, too. Why not?"

While the facials were setting, we took turns in Sara's vibrating foot bath. I was barefoot when the doorbell rang.

"That's the pizza," I said, snatching up the money my mom had left by the phone.

I went to the door and paid for the delivery.

When I walked back into the kitchen, my friends burst out laughing.

"Okay," I said. "What so funny about a super veggie pizza?"

"It's not the pizza," Rebecca said. "It's the green avocado stripe down the middle of your nose!"

Omigosh. I reached for my nose. I had forgotten all about it.

"Please tell me you didn't know the delivery guy," Sara said. "It wasn't some guy from our school?"

"No," I said, relieved. "It was actually a woman, middle-aged. I never saw her before."

"Things to be grateful for," Philomena said, giving me one of her sideways glances. *No,* I thought. She couldn't have had anything to do with who delivered the pizza, could she? That was the problem: Hang out with Philomena long enough and nearly anything can seem like a miracle.

We rinsed off the facials, felt each others' supersmooth skin, then scarfed down the pizza and garlic knots. Finally, we went upstairs to my room for some serious makeover work.

Everyone had brought clothes to try on and trade, and we spread it all out on my bed, along with some magazines that showed "hot new looks to spice up cold winter nights."

I took a quick look at what Phil had brought. Nothing exciting but nothing weird, either: a white button-down shirt, a navy blue cable-knit sweater, a pink T-shirt, and a long multicolored knit scarf.

"Rebecca, you're our first victim, I mean volunteer," Sara said. "The team-shirt look simply isn't working for you anymore. Okay, everyone, we have to put together a superhot outfit for Becca."

"One that will totally blow Scott Hammond away," Andy added.

"But will still make me look like myself," Rebecca pleaded.

"No problem." Sara began picking and choosing pieces, and soon Phil and Andy and I were all making suggestions.

"The wrap sweater is perfect," Sara declared. "You can either wear it with this denim miniskirt with the ragged hem or with these low-rise jeans."

"And, you and I wear the same shoe size," Andy told Rebecca. "So I'll donate my lace-up leather boots to the cause."

"Okay, into the bathroom. Do the skirt first with the boots . . . and don't forget the fishnets." I tossed her a pair of black fishnet stockings, hoping I could sneak them into the pile without an argument.

Rebecca shook her head, laughing. "No way."

"Yes, way. Lindsay Wexler wears them. She wears them all the time."

"I think Rebecca is right." Philomena surprised us all by suddenly speaking up. "I mean . . . Scott didn't ask Lindsay out, did he? He asked Rebecca. She's the one he wants."

"You're right," I said. "You're absolutely right."

"I think I'm going to try the jeans first." Rebecca shot Philomena a grateful smile. "Lindsay is the mini-skirt queen."

While Rebecca changed, we paged through the magazines, looking for good hairstyles.

"Well, what do you think?"

I looked up and saw Rebecca standing in the doorway.

"Awesome!" Sara declared. "Too hot for words."

"Bombshell," Andy agreed, nodding emphatically. "Totally."

"You don't think it's too much?"

"Are you crazy?" Sara demanded.

"It's just . . . after all those years of wearing big, floppy shirts . . . now these clothes show every curve on my body and . . ."

"They look fantastic," Andy assured her. "You look exactly right. You just have to get used to it." Andy jumped up. "I'd say phase one is complete. Phase two: hair and makeup. Step right over to my station." Andy tugged Rebecca over toward my desk.

"What about these?" Sara pulled out a pair of skinny-leg black jeans. "Who wants to try them?"

"Get Philomena to try them," Rebecca said as

Andy settled her under my desk light. "You're next on the catwalk, Phil. Go on. Try them."

Philomena took the jeans, eyeing them dubiously. "These would look good on me? You really think so?"

"Let's see. Go ahead. Try them on," I said.

Sara got up and went over to the bed. "She's got the jeans. . . . What else?"

By the time Philomena went into the bathroom to change, her arms were piled high with an assortment of clothing.

Five minutes later Philomena walked into the room slowly. She looked at us, then stared down at herself.

I felt my jaw actually drop. I couldn't say a word.

Philomena looked so different I probably wouldn't have recognized her.

She wore the skinny jeans with a wide leather belt that had a tooled silver buckle. On top, she'd ended up with a pale blue tank under a black hoodie that slouched off her shoulders. A pair of cowboy boots added an inch or two to her height and made her long, lean legs look even leaner and longer.

"Now that's what I call an amazing transformation," I said. "Phil, you're a hottie!"

Philomena laughed, her face coloring. "Stop it, Grace. I am not."

Sara moved to where Philomena stood and walked in a slow circle around her.

"Hair and makeup next," she announced. "Don't worry. We won't get too carried away. But we have got to do something! Come on, Grace, help me."

Philomena had great hair. It was long and thick, a rich brown color with a slight wave but very smooth and shiny. I brushed it out and tried a few styles, finally ending up with a side part and sexy swoop, set with some gel and a hot roller.

Andy did her makeup, since she was finished with Rebecca. Eye shadow, mascara, lip gloss—the works, but not too much of any of them. When we were done, we just stepped back and gazed at her.

"You guys," Philomena said. "You're making me nervous. You're looking at me like I'm from another planet or something."

"See for yourself," Andy said. She tilted the mirror in Philomena's direction.

Phil gazed at herself in the mirror for what seemed like endless seconds.

"Wow, I really do look different, don't I?"

"I may have gone a little heavy with the mascara," Andy said. "I could tone it down next time."

Philomena turned to her. "I wouldn't change a thing. It's great. I love it."

"You look really good," Rebecca said. "You should dress like that more often."

Philomena opened her mouth to reply. All of a sudden, a strange expression came over her face. The best way I can describe it is to say it was as if she was listening to something. Something only she could hear.

I felt a frisson of pure energy shoot straight down my spine. Was this how it happened? At least some of the time? Was this how Philomena knew she was needed, that she was supposed to help someone?

Had I just witnessed her receiving some sort of message from God?

"Gee," she said, after a moment, her tone bright. "Is it really nine-thirty? I didn't realize it was so late. This has been really great, but I've got to go."

Quickly, she began to gather up her own clothes. Before any of us could get a word in edgewise, she dashed to the bathroom to change.

"I hope we didn't do anything," Rebecca whispered, her eyes on me.

I shook my head. "I don't think so. You guys, when Philomena leaves, we have to follow her. Don't ask me why. We just have to."

Andy's eyes widened. "*Whaat?*" she said, drawing the vowel out long. "Grace, what's going on?"

"It's just—" I knew this wasn't the time for lies. "I have this hunch. I think someone's in trouble, and Philomena is leaving to help them. I know it sounds crazy, but I need to go, too. And I can't get to wherever *that* is if I don't have a car. That means you, Becca. I need you to help me."

"I don't know, Grace," Rebecca said, though I could see she was torn. She was the one who had wanted to follow Philomena the last time around.

"You know how my folks are about me driving at night. They always want me to go where I've told them I'll be, then come straight home. Anything else, they think I'm joyriding."

Philomena emerged from the bathroom, and we quickly broke our huddle. Except for the eye makeup, which she'd left on, she looked like her usual self now. Khaki pants, a red cardigan sweater, and a white cotton turtleneck underneath.

"Thanks again, you guys," she said. "This was great. I really had fun."

"We're going out, too. We'll walk out with you," I said quickly. "My mom got ice cream, but she forgot the hot fudge sauce."

Philomena started down the stairs, and I followed, wondering if my friends would, too. Finally, I heard their footsteps on the stairs behind me. Even though they didn't understand, they were going to support me.

My purse was on the table by the door. I grabbed it and we all walked outside. Philomena climbed into her yellow VW Bug, started up the engine.

We all stood on the sidewalk and waved as she pulled away from the curb.

"Okay, you guys," I said. "Let's go."

"I still don't understand why we're doing this," Andy said. We had been following Philomena for several blocks. "What do you think you're going to find, Grace?"

"It's hard to explain," I said. "I know I'm asking a lot, but, for right now, I just need you to trust me. Please."

A thick silence filled the car. "Sometimes Philomena . . . does things," I felt compelled to go on. "She shows up in places where people need help, just in the nick of time. I'm just wondering if now is one of those times, that's all."

"And what if it is?" Sara asked. "What are we supposed to do about it?"

"Maybe nothing," I said, my tone a little testy. "The point is, I need to *know*. Look up ahead. She's turning. See?"

"I see her." Rebecca turned the wheel, and we rounded a corner. Then her voice became tense. "It looks like Philomena's heading out onto the turnpike. I'm not supposed to drive much on the highway after dark. If my mom finds out, she'll be really mad at me, Grace."

"Just a little farther," I begged. "If nothing happens in the next couple of minutes, we can turn around."

Fortunately, traffic on the turnpike was light. We drove in silence for about three more miles.

"Okay, that's it," Rebecca said. "I'm getting off at the next exit no matter what Philomena does."

"Fine," I said. I knew I didn't have much choice.

That was the moment we all heard it. A sudden squeal of brakes. On the other side of the turnpike, where the traffic was heading in the opposite direction, a car swerved, skidding across the lane next to it.

I watched horrified as another set of headlights swerved—another vehicle trying to get out of the way?—then there was the sickening sound of metal on metal.

"Oh my god! Stop the car," I yelled. "Rebecca, you've got to pull over on the shoulder.

"What about following—"

"Just stop now!"

Breathlessly, Rebecca guided the car onto the shoulder of the highway and stopped.

I opened the door. Around us, I could hear the sound of cars speeding by. Our side of the highway seemed completely unaffected by the accident.

"Grace, what are you doing?" Andy asked.

"I'm going to go over there and see if anyone needs help," I said.

"You're going to cross the highway at night? Are you crazy?" Sara demanded.

"I have to," I said "Use your cell. Call 911. Get help. I'll be back as soon as I can."

"That could take—a while." Rebecca sounded panicked. "I don't want to sit here all night."

"Then go," I said. "I'll be fine."

"Grace, going over there could be dangerous," Andy said.

I put a hand on her arm, trying not to notice the way my fingers trembled. "I know, Andy. I know. I'll be careful, I promise. I just need to see if there's anything I can do."

"Then I'm coming with you," she said, her jaw set.

I opened the passenger door and got out. Then Sara pushed the seat forward and followed.

"We're all coming with you." Becca grabbed a flashlight from the glove compartment and came out after us.

We waited until our side of the highway had cleared, and dashed across to the median.

The scene in front of us was straight out of a nightmare. The car that had swerved across the lanes was a small sedan. It had hit an SUV almost directly head on, and both had spun onto the far shoulder of the road. Why both vehicles hadn't gone up in flames was a mystery.

"Look!" Andy suddenly pointed as she snapped her cell closed.

Someone, maybe the driver of the SUV, had been thrown clear and was lying near the median. In the lanes in front of us traffic had slowed to a crawl, and the bright headlights cast a harsh white glare over everything.

"Okay, listen up, guys," I said. "This is what we're going to do. Becca, your mom has flares in the trunk of her car, right?"

"Absolutely," Becca said. She sounded calmer now. "My mom's a total safety nut."

"Can you go back to the car and get them? Then you and Andy can set them up to keep people a safe distance away. Sara and I will check on the passengers."

Becca handed me her flashlight. "Remember not to move anyone," she said as we began to move off.

We went toward the person who lay near the median. She was a young blond-haired woman. She couldn't have been more than about twenty-five. As Sara and I knelt down beside her, she began to moan.

"It's going to be all right," I said. I was afraid to touch her, afraid to make her injuries worse, but I put all the reassurance and positive energy I could into my voice.

"We called 911," I told her. "Help is on the way."

"Danny," the woman said, her voice a thin reed of sound. "My son, Danny."

I looked up and met Sara's eyes. If there was a kid, he was probably in the backseat of the SUV.

"I'll go check on him," I said. "Stay with her, Sara."

Again, I waited until it was safe to cross. Then I darted over to the SUV. The back passenger door hung open. I shined the flashlight inside. I could see a child's car seat, still in place, the form in it, unmoving.

Oh, no. Please, God, no, I thought.

"Hey, Danny, is that you?" I said. I leaned in, being careful not to jostle him. He was maybe four years old. "My name is Grace. I'm going to stay right here with you."

All of a sudden, the little boy opened his eyes, fastening them on mine. He opened his mouth as if to cry, but no sound came out.

"It's going to be okay, Danny," I said. He might not be crying, but I could hear the wail of sirens now. "You hear that?" I went on. "That means the police are on their way. They'll be here any minute. Then you can see your mom."

I have no idea how long it actually took for the cops to arrive. I only know I stood beside that SUV, talking nonstop. Telling Danny over and over again the hope in my heart: That everything would be all right.

"We'll take things from here, ma'am," I suddenly heard a voice.

I looked up. A young cop was standing by my side.

"This is Danny," I said, my voice hoarse. "His mom—"

"Is receiving medical attention," the cop filled in. "You and your friends did a great job. If you'll just step away from the vehicle, so the medics can go to work."

"Sure, okay," I said. Now that help was here, I was starting to feel a little dazed. As I finally stepped away, Danny began to cry.

"Hey, Danny, it's going to be just fine," I said. "See? I'm not going very far. The doctor is going to get you out, and then he's going to take you to your mom."

The medics moved in then, and the cop gently steered me away from the SUV.

"If I could just have your name," the young cop said.

"What? Oh, Grace. My name is Grace Stanley. My friends are Andy Chin, Sara Kramer, and Rebecca Giomi."

"And is she a friend of yours, too?" He nodded toward the shoulder of the highway. A slender young woman knelt there, holding the hand of a man whose face was streaked with blood.

I wasn't even surprised.

"Yes," I said. "She's my friend, too. That's Philomena Cantos."

The cop made a notation in his notebook, then looked up. "I just want you to know, Grace," he said. "You and your friends made a big difference here tonight. You got these people the help they needed fast. You should all be very proud of that."

I nodded. What he said was true, but I felt funny taking the credit. After all, we never would have been here if not for Philomena.

"You all should go home," the cop said. "If we need further statements, we'll be in touch."

I nodded and turned toward Rebecca's car. The others were already there, leaning against it wearily.

"Are you guys okay?" I asked.

"We're fine," Andy said.

"Actually, I feel kind of lucky," Becca admitted. She gave me a quick hug. "That was a smart call, Grace. Those people were in serious trouble. It felt good to be able to help them."

Nine

"THERE'S JUST ONE THING I want to know," Sara said on Sunday morning. It was about 11:30 and the four of us were gathered at Big Drip, our favorite coffeehouse. Rebecca was giving us the lowdown on her date with Scott Hammond.

So far, she had been keeping us in suspense about one all-important point.

"Don't tell me." I rolled my eyes. "You want to know if they would recommend the movie."

"Graaace," Sara groaned. Across the table from me, I could see that both Andy and Rebecca's eyes were dancing with laughter. "I want to know if he kissed her, of course."

"Of course is right," Andy said at once. "The real question is, how was it?" She fixed her eyes on Rebecca. "So spill, Giomi. You're not leaving here until you do, so don't even think about getting out of it."

"It was . . . fantastic," Rebecca said with a sigh.

"The whole evening was fantastic, from start to finish. I had a really great time."

"Okay, but tell us about the kiss," Sara insisted.

Becca blushed. If it had been Sara's date, we would have gotten a moment-by-moment dramatic reenactment. Becca isn't like that, though. She's a lot more shy.

"She just did," I intervened. "Don't be a pain, Sara." I gave Rebecca's shoulder a squeeze. "I'd say fantastic is a pretty good place to start."

Becca shot me a quick, grateful smile.

"Okay," Sara said. "Let's move on. When are you going to see him again?"

"Tomorrow," Rebecca answered promptly.

"Tomorrow. Wow, that's quick," Andy said.

Sara made a fist and rapped on Andy's head with her knuckles. "Anybody in there? Hello . . . Tomorrow is Monday. School. Chem lab. Of course she'll see him on Monday. I'm asking when she'll *see* him again."

Rebecca took a breath. "I honestly don't know." She gave an unhappy shrug. "Scott kissed me good night . . ." She shot a glance in Sara's direction. "Then he said something like, I'll call you, or I'll see you around. In other words, something highly unspecific."

"He could still call," Andy said quickly. "You just went out last night. It's only Sunday morning."

"I know that," Rebecca said. "I know, it's just . . ."

"Guys are unspecific," Sara said. "It's a well-documented fact."

"Think about how your brothers communicate, Becca," I suggested. "You know how twisted that can get."

Rebecca nodded, her expression a little calmer. "Yeah, I guess. Thanks, you guys. I guess I just needed some reassurance."

"Scott likes you," I said. "I know it."

"There's something else I want to talk about," Rebecca said, her tone tensing up again, as if she were steeling herself. "I want to talk about Friday night. About what happened when we followed Philomena."

"I want to talk about why we did that in the first place," Sara put in quickly.

"You and me both," Andy nodded. "What's the deal with Philomena? What's going on, Grace?"

I had known this moment would come. But that didn't make answering the questions any easier, particularly since I had at least one of my own. Such as: How on earth did you tell your oldest friends that you thought your newest one had been sent to help you by a higher power? Not just any higher power. The highest one there is.

"You all remember the beginning of the school year," I said, slowly. Maybe it was best to ease into this.

"Who could forget it?" Sara said. "To put it bluntly, you were a mess."

"Sara," Andy chided gently.

"No, Sara's right," I said. "I *was* a mess. And, much as I appreciate all of you, the truth is that the real reason I got through it was because Philomena and I became friends. She helped me come back to my life. To remember who I am."

There was a beat of silence.

"I've got to say that hurts a little," Rebecca confessed. "The fact that it was someone brand new who got you through and not any of us. We tried to help."

"You *did* help," I said. "But what I was going through needed something special. Something only Philomena could give. She's not like other people, you guys. She told me . . ." I took a breath. "She told me she was *sent* to help me—and I believe it's true."

Sara made a puzzled face. "Sent," she echoed. "What is that supposed to mean? Who sent her?"

This was it: the moment of truth. I spoke mine.

"God," I said.

Complete silence fell around the table. Everyone was staring at me like I'd suddenly grown an extra head. And all of a sudden, I found myself praying. I guess that's what you'd call it.

Please, please believe me, I thought. *Please try to understand.*

Sara's eyes narrowed. "You've been drinking again, haven't you?" she asked.

"Sara!" Rebecca exclaimed. "What's the matter with you? Why are you being so hostile?"

"How can you even ask that?" Sara demanded. "Listen to her! She just told us she thought Philomena Cantos was sent by God. How far out there is that? Don't you think I have the right to feel a little concerned and upset?"

"Of course you have the right to feel concerned. We all feel concerned," Andy said. "But Grace is our friend. There's no need to attack her for telling us what she believes." She shot me a look. "Even if it is pretty out there."

"Look, I know it's a lot to swallow. I didn't do so well at first, myself," I said. "But haven't any of you ever felt things you couldn't quite explain around Phil?"

"I have," Rebecca admitted. "You know that. But it's a pretty big jump from that to believing she was sent by God."

"What makes you think Philomena was sent?" Andy asked. "Did she say she was?"

"As a matter of fact, she did," I said.

"But that doesn't mean you have to believe it!" Sara exclaimed. "I'm glad if Philomena helped you. Don't get me wrong. But all this other stuff . . ." She threw her hands up in the air in a typical Sara dramatic gesture. "I'm sorry, but I just don't understand how you could fall for what sounds like such an obvious scam."

"It's not a scam, Sara. It's the truth," I said. "Besides, what would Philomena have to gain even if it was a scam? It's not like I'm super popular, or super rich. There's absolutely no reason for her to lie."

"And haven't you ever felt . . . I don't know . . . *different* when Philomena is around?" Rebecca suddenly jumped. "Like there's this *energy* coming from her, almost as if she's channeling something. Like on Saturday night."

"That's it. That's it exactly," I said. "I felt something coming from her—or through her—when she suddenly announced she had to take off. I just knew that she was leaving to help someone. That's what she's here for. To help. Not just me. Other people, too."

Andy frowned, as if trying to recall an elusive answer on a math test. "She was there, wasn't she? At the accident."

I nodded. "On the shoulder, on the far side of the road," I said. "I saw her kneeling beside one of the other victims."

"But how did she get over there?" Andy asked. "She was ahead of us, and we didn't see her pull off. The next place she could have turned around was five miles up the road. That means she would have to drive ten miles total, and the traffic on the other side of the road was completely snarled. We didn't see her VW on our side of the highway and—"

"That's what I mean," I interrupted. "Ever since I met Phil, things happen that I can't possibly explain. At least not in any logical way. But they always seem to involve the same thing: helping someone."

"I saw a news report this morning," Sara said slowly. "The reporter was doing a follow-up on the accident. Everyone survived."

"But there's no proof that's because of Philomena," Andy pointed out.

"No," I agreed. "But that doesn't mean I'm wrong. I even believe that it was no coincidence that I wanted to follow her—and you all were willing to come along. I think we were all needed there, and somehow, thanks to Philomena, we all showed up."

"God sent her, and she sent us?" Sara inquired, but her tone didn't sound quite so hostile now. Instead it sounded . . . intrigued.

"Maybe," I said. "Just tell me this: Do you think I'm completely nuts?"

"Of course we do," Andy said at once, but I could see that she was smiling. "That's not the same thing as saying we don't believe you, Grace. Or at least, that we don't realize that *you* believe what you've told us about Philomena."

She glanced around the table. "I don't know

about the rest of you, but I'm going to need a little time to think this over."

"That's fair enough," I said. "The only thing I ask is that you keep an open mind."

And maybe, I thought, an open heart. But I kept that wish to myself.

By the time Monday and the fifth-period yearbook staff meeting rolled around, I had most of my caricatures drawn. I had spent the rest of Sunday working on them.

The yearbook meetings were always super informal. Mostly, it was just a chance for the staff to get together and talk about what needed to be done. No sooner had I taken my seat than Philomena walked in. She came over and sat down next to me at once.

"It's so great to see you here, Grace," she said. "Did you decide to rejoin the yearbook staff after all?"

"Not officially, at least not yet," I replied. "But I suppose I might as well. I've been doing some drawings for Ms. Kaplanski."

I rotated my sketch pad, so that she could see some of the drawings.

"Oh, I love these," Philomena exclaimed. "They're awesome."

She's sounding more like the rest of us every day, I thought. *And looking like us, too.* Today's outfit was sort of halfway between her previous geek look and the superchic look we had given her at spa night. A pair of form-fitting jeans and a turtleneck. The turtleneck was a little baggy, but the jeans were dynamite.

"Philomena," I said. I leaned in closer and cast a quick look around the room. Everybody else was concentrating on their own stuff. Nobody was paying attention to Phil and me. "Can I ask you something?"

"You can ask anything you like," Philomena said, but I caught the inflection in her voice. Just because I could ask didn't mean I would get an answer. At least, not a straight one.

"Did you know what was going to happen on Friday night? Did you know there was going to be an accident?"

"No." Philomena shook her head at once. "I can't predict or foresee the future, Grace. I just help."

"Then why did you leave spa night so suddenly? I saw the look on your face. You knew something was up." I waited a beat, then went on. "We followed you. That's why we were there when the accident happened. That's why *we* were there to help."

"Then that's what was supposed to happen," Philomena said at once. "That's why I left."

"Yes, but what if we hadn't followed?" I insisted. "What would have happened then?"

"Something else." Philomena's words sounded

dismissive, but I knew they weren't. I made a frustrated sound.

"The universe is filled with possibilities," she went on, "all sort of streaming together at the same time. None of us can see all of them. That's why individual actions and decisions are so important. They're the things that make the difference.

"When I left the party, that opened up one set of possibilities. Your decision to follow opened up another. I can't tell you what would have happened if you and your friends hadn't been at the scene of that accident because you were. That's the path you chose."

"Has anyone ever told you talking to you is like peeling an onion?" I inquired. "No matter how hard I try, I never get through all the layers."

Philomena gave a quick laugh.

"Just so long as I don't smell like one."

I got to English early and saved a seat for Rebecca in the back row so we could talk. She spotted me and dropped down in her chair.

"So?" I asked. "How are things with Scott?"

"I saw him in chem lab. He came over to talk and was really nice. He said he had fun on Saturday night."

"Well, okay, that's good."

Rebecca shook her head. "Not good enough. He hasn't said a thing about going out again. Though I overheard him talking to Mitch Sanderson and Grant Hodge in the hall. A bunch of them are going to the basketball game Friday night. It sounded like something they've been planning for a while."

Ms. Kaplanski began to write on the board, and Becca and I both opened our books to at least look like we were paying attention.

"I'll tell you what I think," I said in a low voice. "I think you should go to the game on Friday night."

Rebecca twisted a strand of hair around one finger, a gesture she makes when she's nervous. "You don't think that's—you know—too obvious? I don't want to look like I'm stalking him, or something."

"What's stalking about going to a game? We go to them all the time. You should definitely go, just to show your face. I'll bet Lindsay and her crew will be there."

"That figures."

"And I'll go with you," I offered, though basketball was not my favorite sport.

Becca's expression brightened at once. "Would you really? You hate basketball."

"Not as much as Andy and Sara," I said.

"This is true," Rebecca said. Impulsively, she leaned over to give me a hug, then scooted back as Ms. Kaplanski shot a look in our direction. "Now

I'll have something to look forward to even if seeing Scott is a bust."

"Anything for a friend," I said. And turned my attention to the chalkboard.

I worked a closing shift at AR that night, my very first one. This meant that Ms. Newberry really trusted me. Usually, only employees who had worked there a lot longer got to help with closing up.

Each section of the store had its own cash register. After we closed for the day, the manager of each department would do the money stuff while the floor staff straightened and restocked.

Ms. Newberry usually cashed out the embellishments department herself. Along with the food section, I think it was her favorite part of the store.

It was different being in Alternate Realities after all the customers were gone. There's something both eerie and peaceful about a store after hours. I kept thinking of all those movies where the mannequins and toys come to life.

I knew Jackson was working, too, though I had only managed to glimpse him a couple of times that day. The closer we got to the end of November and Thanksgiving, the busier the store got. But the few times I had seen him, he looked distracted. He hardly even said hello.

The thought that maybe something had happened between us had crossed my mind. Not that I could figure out what it was. Last time we were together, things had been totally great. Maybe he was just worried about the big Battle of the Bands competition, which was coming up that weekend.

I finished the last of my assignments, rearranging a display of napkins and placemats that had gotten totally messed up by a couple of unsupervised toddlers.

"Anything else you need me to do?" I asked Ms. Newberry as I approached the cash register desk.

Ms. Newberry glanced up from where she was putting things in a deposit pouch. "What? Oh, no, thank you, Grace." She gave the repaired display an approving look. "That looks very nice."

The trill of a phone interrupted us. It was the one in the stockroom, which has a special ring. Ms. Newberry always picks that one up.

"Oh, dear. I'm going to have to get that," she said. "Do me a favor, will you, Grace, and finish writing up these checks? Just fill in the amounts on the deposit slip, then put it in the bag with the cash."

"Will do."

Ms. Newberry walked briskly toward the back of the shop, and I began working on the deposit slip.

"Hey, check you out," I heard Jackson's voice say. "What's up with you? Did you get a promotion?"

"Not very likely," I said, looking up and grinning at him. "It's just that Ms. Newberry had to take a call in the stockroom."

I went back to my job, concentrating on filling in the check amounts correctly, aware that Jackson had come to stand beside me. I put the checks into the deposit envelope, stacking them behind the cash.

"Oh, cool," I said. "Look, here's a hundred dollar bill. The only other time I've seen one of these was the year our grandparents sent Matt and me one each for Christmas."

"That Benjamin Franklin," Jackson said. "What a good-looking guy."

I gave a gurgle of laughter as I put the bill back in the envelope. "You are so lame," I said.

"You'd like to think so."

Just at that moment, I heard Ms. Newberry call, "Grace, could you come here a moment, please?"

"Sure, Ms. Newberry," I called back. I felt my stomach clench. Should I put the deposit bag away, or leave it on the counter? The store was closed. There was no reason to put it away. Except that Jackson was there. Jackson who had taken money from the store before. Who'd put it back and promised me he'd never steal again.

If I locked the deposit bag up, would he think I didn't trust him? After all we'd been through, was that really what I wanted?

"I'll be right back," I said. I took off toward the stockroom, leaving the deposit bag on the counter.

Ms. Newberry needed me to check the supply of a particular soda we stock. It was all the way back in the cooler, and, though the phone was portable, it got lousy reception in the fridge.

I finished the stock check, gave Ms. Newberry the information. She'd just finished up her conversation.

"Oh, dear. Now I'm running late," she said, as she peered at her watch. "Do me one more favor, will you, dear? Go get that deposit and put it in my office. I'll take it to the bank tomorrow morning instead of tonight."

"Sure," I said. I headed back out to embellishments. Jackson was still there, leaning against the far side of the counter.

"I'll be ready to go in just a minute," I said.

"Actually," he said, "I have to run. Can I call you tonight?"

"Okay. No problem," I said, suddenly embarrassed. I shouldn't have just assumed we were going to walk home together. Still, why had he come over in the first place if we weren't?

"Talk to you later then," he said. He turned on one heel and walked quickly toward the front of the store.

I picked up the deposit bag. I guess I was rattled,

or maybe not paying enough attention to what I was doing, but the bag slipped from my fingers and fell to the floor. All the cash and checks in the deposit cascaded out. Quickly, I knelt to scoop them up and put everything back in order.

It wasn't until I was actually stuffing everything back into the bag that what my hands had discovered filtered through to my mind.

The hundred dollar bill was gone.

I didn't know what to do. Ms. Newberry had already left. I set the deposit envelope on her desk. Then I left the store quickly, my mind blazing. I was furious with Jackson and almost as furious with myself. *How could I have let this happen?*

I had trusted Jackson, totally fallen for him. And he had lied. Stolen money after he swore he would never do it again. Not only had he stolen from Ms. Newberry after he promised me he wouldn't, he did it right under my nose. Did it in a way that could jeopardize my job, as well as his. After all, I was the one responsible for that deposit envelope. When Ms. Newberry found out the money was missing, guess who was going to be blamed.

He used you, Grace, I thought. *He took advantage of the fact that you care about him.*

Was he counting on me *not* to expose him if I discovered what was going on? Was that what our relationship had been about? Was it possible he didn't really care for me at all?

I stopped at a curb, waiting for the light to change, and heard the quick tap of a car horn. There was no mistaking that sound. It was definitely a VW.

Philomena, I thought.

"Hey, Grace. Need a lift?" she called.

Do I ever, I thought. I got in and closed the door. The light changed, and Philomena continued driving.

"You look upset," she said after a moment. "Is anything wrong?"

"You were right." I hated the bitterness in my voice but I couldn't help it.

"About what?"

"Try asking what you're *not* right about," I said. "I'm thinking that list would be shorter."

"Grace—"

"Jackson is stealing," I blurted out. "Again. I have proof this time. I practically caught him red-handed. It was bad enough when I thought he would just get himself in trouble. But now he could screw me up, too. He took a hundred dollars from a deposit I was working on. If Ms. Newberry notices the money is missing, she'll think I took it. I could be arrested, lose my job."

Philomena was silent for a moment, negotiating a corner.

"What are you going to do?" she asked quietly.

"I don't know!" I cried out. "That's just the point! I almost want to turn him in. I can't even remember the last time I was so furious."

"Almost?"

I looked at her in disbelief. "If I turn him in, he'll be arrested. He could go to jail. He won't go to college. He'll never be able to get a decent job. I will be completely wrecking his life—and Sam's. Sam is really dependent on Jackson now that their parents are such a mess. So I'll be totally destroying their family. And I'll lose him," I added more quietly. "For good."

"So . . . even after what he did, you still want to . . . go on seeing him?" Phil asked.

"I don't know," I said. "What I want is for Jackson not to be messing up at all. But I guess I can't have that, can I?"

Philomena was silent. Big surprise.

Then something else occurred to me. "You wanted me to work at AR. You knew Jackson was the one who needed help. Even though you tried to warn me not to get involved with him. But you set me up for it all along."

Phil sent me a sideways glance. "Are you ever going to believe me when I tell you that I can't predict the future? I did sense Jackson needed help.

And I knew you would be able to help him. The rest, though—how it played out—those were the choices you and Jackson made."

"Back up a second," I said, feeling a flicker of hope. "What do you mean, you knew I could help him? If that's true, then just tell me how. *How* can I help him?"

Another silence.

"Grace, I know this is hard. Concentrate on what you can do that will really, truly help Jackson. The truth is going to have to come out. Help Jackson find the way to be true to himself. If you can find a way to do that, you'll have done what's right."

I sighed. Actually, I had to admit Philomena had been a lot more specific than she usually is. And talking to her did make me feel a little better.

"It's those possibilities you were talking about, isn't it?" I asked as she pulled up in front of my house.

Philomena nodded as she put the car in park.

"That's what we do, Grace. We create possibilities. Think of it like opening a whole bunch of doors. Which one Jackson goes through is up to him. All you can do is to make sure he understands there's a choice."

My brief flicker of hope died. "You think I should turn him in, don't you?"

"You know I can't tell you what to do."

"Fine. I just want to know one more thing," I said, opening the door. "Does any of this ever get any easier?"

Philomena gave a quick, surprised laugh. "That's a good question," she said. "I'm going to have to think about it."

"Me, too," I said as I got out of the car, and she drove off.

When I got inside, my mother was on the phone in the kitchen, talking to a client.

". . . it's three bedrooms on the specs, but the study on the first floor really makes it four. . . . The hot water heater is about three years old. . . . Sure, I can check on that for you. . . ."

"I'm home," I yelled out.

I went upstairs to my room, flopped on my bed, and stared up at the ceiling.

Possibilities. Choices. Chances, I thought.

How many was I willing to give Jackson? There was the possibility, a very definite one, that I would give in to my anger, my sense of betrayal, and just plain rat him out. That would definitely open a few unexpected doors.

And how many would it close? I wondered. For sure he would get fired. He might even go to jail. Was that what I wanted?

Why, Jackson? I thought.

And suddenly, I knew what my answer would be, at least in the short run. I knew what was right. I wouldn't do anything until I'd had a chance to ask Jackson that very question myself.

As far as I was concerned, he owed me an explanation. And I was going to make absolutely certain that I got one.

Ten

"GRACE, TELEPHONE," my mom called out.

It was several hours later, after dinner. My dad had to work late, which meant Mom and I were on our own. We ordered in from our favorite Chinese takeout place. Afterward, Mom settled in front of the TV to veg and I went up to my room.

I tried to do some sketching, but nothing worked and I gave up. The truth is, all I was really doing was waiting for Jackson to call.

"Thanks, Mom, I've got it," I called back.

I waited until I heard the click that meant she had hung up the downstairs extension.

"Hello?"

"Grace, it's Jackson," his voice said. "Can we talk?"

"You bet we can," I said. "And not over the phone. I know what you did this afternoon, Jackson. What I don't know is why. I want to be able to look you right in the eye when you try to explain."

There was a heavy pause. "I have a good reason," he said.

"I hope so."

"Just let me explain, Grace," he said. And all of a sudden, I could hear the panic in his voice. "Just hear me out. That's all I ask," he went on, his voice urgent now.

"Where do you want to meet?"

"How about down at Max's?"

It was the local burger joint. Far enough away from school so that we probably wouldn't see anyone we knew.

"Okay," I said. "I'll see you in a few."

I grabbed a jacket and headed out. When I got to Max's, it was clear the dinner rush was over. There were a few kids playing the couple of video games in the back, but most of the tables were empty. I spotted Jackson in a booth at the back and slid in opposite him.

"You want anything?" he asked, as I sat down.

"How about an explanation," I said. "What the hell is going on?"

"You're not going to get in trouble," he said quickly. A nice promise, not that he could keep it. And it didn't answer my question at all. "I swear it. I'd never do that to you."

"You already have, Jackson!" I cried. His eyes widened, as if he was afraid somebody else would overhear. I leaned in and spoke more softly. "If Ms. Newberry notices that money is missing, who do you think she's going to think stole it? I was the one she asked to work on that deposit, not you. I'm the obvious choice, no matter how much she likes me."

Jackson's face turned pale. "That's not what I want . . . I would never . . ."

"But that's what you did. Jackson, stop and think."

A spasm of irritation crossed his face. "I have a mother. You don't have to sound just like her."

I ignored that. "You promised me you wouldn't do this again," I told him. "You promised you were done. Now I need to know why you lied."

"It's Battle of the Bands," he said. "We registered, sent in a demo . . . I thought we were all set to go. Then, yesterday, I got some stuff in the mail. There's this extra fee they don't tell you about up front. If we don't fill a certain number of seats when we play, we have to pay the promoters for them. And uh . . . the Daily Dose has not exactly sold out the house."

I felt my stomach sink. "So you stole the money to cover the fee?"

"It's just for a couple of days, Grace. But I'm going to pay it back—by Monday. I figured it out. All we have to do is sell a bunch of tickets to our friends and family and we'll get it back."

"Jackson . . . I can see how this fee seemed to tally unfair. I can even see how desperate you might have felt to just pay it, and not lose your chance in the contest. But you can't keep taking the easy way out."

"Look, Grace," he said. "All we have to do is sit tight. If Ms. Newberry asks about the deposit, just tell her the truth. You put that hundred dollar bill in the bag."

"And if she asks me if I know what happened to it after that?" I said. "What am I supposed to do then. Lie?"

He didn't answer for a moment.

"That *is* what you want me to do, isn't it?" I asked softly. "You want me to cover for you."

"It's just for a couple of days," he said again, his tone completely defensive now. "Just until Monday. I can bring the money back, slip it in the drawer. It will all seem like a big misunderstanding. You only thought it went into the deposit envelope. It'll be 'all's well that ends well.'"

I slid from the booth, my heart pounding so loud it made my ears ring. Cold, clammy sweat seemed to drip right down my spine.

"I can't believe you're saying those things," I said. "You know I can't do that. I thought you cared about me. I guess I was wrong."

"Grace!" His voice was low and pleading.

"We're done." I said. "Good luck with the band contest, Jackson. I hope you win big. It's pretty clear that's what you care about."

"Grace, wait—don't go," he said. But by then it was too late.

I was running for the door.

Friday passed in this sort of weird limbo. I didn't see Jackson at all at school. I had the afternoon off from Alternate Realities, though I half expected to find a call from Ms. Newberry on the answering machine when I got home. Surely, she must have turned in the deposit by now. A quick count of the cash would be all that was needed to show something was missing.

But there was nothing. Nothing at all.

Did this let me off the hook? If I didn't call Ms. Newberry and tell her what I knew, was I doing exactly what I'd accused Jackson of wanting me to do? Was I covering for him?

Of course you are, Grace, I thought. But even knowing that, I still couldn't bring myself to pick up the phone and call Ms. Newberry. Not yet, anyhow.

I knew, beyond a shadow of a doubt, that what Jackson was doing was wrong. But going to Ms. Newberry didn't seem like quite the right choice, either. Telling the truth about what happened should be Jackson's job, not mine.

By the time the end of the day rolled around, I was completely exhausted. The last thing I wanted to do was to go to a basketball game—but I had promised Rebecca, and I couldn't let her down.

The basketball game was a total scene, as usual. The bleachers were packed, and we finally scrambled up to find seats way on top. No sooner had we settled onto the hard seats than Rebecca began to scan the crowd for Scott.

"There he is. I see him. Right down there." She gave me a poke with her elbow. "See, down there on the left."

"I see them."

Scott and his buds were sitting a couple rows up from the floor, mid-court. And sitting in the row directly in front of them were Lindsay, Dana, and Morgan. Lindsay kept turning around to flirt with Scott, leaning close and putting her hand on his knee.

I felt Rebecca stiffen beside me as the two teams ran out onto the court.

"It probably doesn't mean anything," I told her. "Lindsay's just being Lindsay. She's not used to losing."

"Neither am I," Rebecca said.

The game started at a quick tempo and was fierce almost from the start. The players seemed to move in a blur. Dana Sloan's brother, Dylan, a forward, was scoring like mad, soaking up most of the glory.

Finally, the buzzer sounded half-time. The crowd surged to its feet, everyone heading for the bathrooms or refreshment stands at once. It took Rebecca and me a while to get down to the gym floor, then out into the lobby. It was supercrowded by the time we got there, but we spotted Scott and his friends in one of the drink lines.

Lindsay and crew were nowhere in sight.

"How do I look?" Becca asked me.

"Perfect," I replied. Becca was wearing a ballet-dancer-type top, long-sleeved and close-fitting, with straight-leg jeans. "Now get over there and say hello before Lindsay shows up. If he asks you to sit with him, say yes."

"What about you?"

"I'll be fine."

She squared her shoulders. "Okay, here goes."

I watched Rebecca make her way toward Scott and Scott smile as he caught sight of her.

Three minutes later, Scott and Rebecca were sitting together in the common area. Rebecca was talking animatedly about something, her cheeks slightly flushed, her eyes shining. As I watched, Scott reached out to touch her cheek, moving a strand of hair from her eyes.

I swallowed hard, remembering how Jackson had once touched me that way. Oh god, but I was going to miss that.

Just then, I felt a gust as someone flew out of the girls' bathroom. Lindsay Wexler. She scanned the lobby, spotted Scott and Rebecca, and headed straight toward them.

Lindsay had taken only a few steps when this guy suddenly materialized, going full steam, from out of the crowd. In one hand, he held the biggest cup of soda I had ever seen.

He crashed right into Lindsay, sending the entire contents of his cup streaming down her front. Lindsay fell back with a cry, then as the guy tried frantically to apologize, she spun around and dashed out, followed by Dana and Morgan.

"Grace!" It was Becca, just behind me. "Scott wants us to come and sit with him," she said. "Is that all right?"

"You go," I said. "I think I'm going to head out. I've got a headache."

"If you're sure . . ." Becca said.

"Absolutely," I smiled. "Have a great time and I'll talk to you tomorrow. Nice to see you, Scott."

I watched as they walked hand in hand back into

the crowded gym. At least somebody's love life was going right.

It was just past nine when I got home from the game. My parents were out, at a movie, but Philomena's familiar yellow Bug was parked in front of the house.

The decision I'd been avoiding at the game was suddenly right back in front of me, flashing in neon letters. I sighed, opened the passenger door, and slid into the front seat. "Hey, Phil," I said.

Her dark eyes searched my face. "I was wondering how you were doing."

"I'm okay," I said.

"You're okay about Jackson?"

I answered in a monotone. "We talked. He admitted he stole the money. He said he's going to repay it by Monday."

"And that's all right with you?" she asked, her voice tinged with disbelief.

"No, it's not all right." Suddenly, I was furious again, furious that I had lost Jackson, and Philomena was sitting there acting righteous. "Nothing's all right. I told him it was over between us. Are you happy now?"

"Of course not," she said. "You know that's not the whole story."

I shut my eyes for a second, blinking back the tears. "I know the right thing to do is to turn him in. But I can't do it. I—"

"I know this is hard for you—"

"You don't know." I was shouting now. "Have you ever had a boyfriend? Have you ever been in love? Can you honestly tell me you know the first thing about it?"

Philomena touched my arm gently, and I felt that warmth sweep through me.

"I never had a boyfriend," she said simply.

"Did you ever want one?" I asked, my voice quavering.

One edge of Philomena's mouth turned up. "I did. But I think what I really wanted was just to feel loved."

"What happened?"

"I realized I *was* loved," she said, as if it were the most obvious thing in the world. "And when I did, that need went away, and in its place . . . I found I needed to help others."

"I'm not like that," I said.

"Maybe not exactly," she said. "But I think you have a gift for helping people, Grace. You just may be Jackson's best chance."

I shook my head. "No, Jackson's got to be his own best chance."

She smiled then. "Yeah, how about that?"

Eleven

I WOKE UP SATURDAY MORNING filled with dread. I knew I couldn't hide from the truth. I had to tell Ms. Newberry what happened—even though it meant I would lose Jackson forever. But what I really wanted to do was to pull the covers back over my head and close my eyes.

Today was the Battle of the Bands.

I hadn't spoken to Jackson since the night he stole that hundred dollars from the store. Ever since, I'd expected Ms. Newberry to call. She hadn't. But instead of making me feel better, it made me feel worse. The silence felt ominous, somehow. The day seemed to stretch out before me like a long, dark tunnel.

"Grace," my mother called up the stairs. "Breakfast! You better get down before your dad eats all the bacon. I'm trying to save you some, but you know how he is."

I tossed aside the covers and got out of bed. I

didn't really care whether or not my dad ate all the bacon. But anything was better than lying in bed worrying about what was going to happen next.

And what wasn't.

About halfway through breakfast, the phone rang. From across the table, I saw my dad frown. It wasn't all that early, but my dad has all these internal rules about when it's too early or late to call. And he hates it when someone calls during meals, even when he lets the machine pick up the call.

"If that's one of your friends, I expect you to call them back later, Grace," he said as I got up to answer the phone.

I glanced at the caller ID display.

Alternate Realities.

My heart leapt into my throat and my stomach sank, all at the same time.

"It's the store," I said. "I'd better pick up."

My father rattled his newspaper but didn't object.

"Hello?"

"Oh, Grace. That is your voice, isn't it?" Ms. Newberry's own distinctive one came on the line.

"Yes, it's me. Hello, Ms. Newberry." My drama teacher would have been proud. I actually managed to sound calm.

"Do you need something?" I asked.

"As a matter of fact, I do," Ms. Newberry said.

"We've had a staff member call in sick at the last moment. I know you don't usually work today, but I'm hoping you can come in to cover the shift."

My heart settled back into my chest, then began to beat double time. Was that really all Ms. Newberry wanted, or was this just a convenient way of getting me to come in to the store?

For a moment, I was tempted to say I couldn't come in. I knew my mom was going to church to help with the annual coat drive. And I knew my dad really wanted me to log some volunteer hours for my college application. I could tell Ms. Newberry no with a perfectly legitimate excuse.

I could take the easy way out.

Which is exactly what you've been doing, Grace, I suddenly realized. It hadn't felt easy. In fact, I had been feeling pretty awful. I'd been on pins and needles for days, wondering what would happen next. Arguing with myself—and Philomena—over what I should and shouldn't do. But, standing in the kitchen, clutching the phone in my hand, one thing suddenly became crystal clear.

The longer I put off dealing with what had happened at Alternate Realities, the longer the whole awful mess would hang over me. Doing nothing wasn't the answer, either.

"Sure, I can come in," I said. "What time do you need me?"

"Well," Ms. Newberry said, "Shannon was supposed to help open the store, so it would be nice if you could get here as soon as possible. I'll understand if you can't make it right away, of course. This is pretty late notice."

"I'll be there in an hour," I promised.

"That will be just fine, Grace." Ms. Newberry's voice warmed. "Thanks so much. I'll see you then."

She ended the call. I stood for a moment with the silent phone in my hand, then slowly put it back into the cradle.

Well, that's that, I thought. Either I would still have a job at the end of the day, or I wouldn't.

There was only one way to find out.

An hour later, I was walking through the doors of Alternate Realities. The day had turned cold and rainy. In the dim light, the harvest window I'd created seemed to glow with welcoming color.

Now the question was, would I be welcome?

It wasn't the only question, of course. The bigger one was this: If by some miracle Ms. Newberry hadn't discovered the missing money, what was I going to do about it?

If I told her, I could ruin Jackson's life, or at least make it seriously more complicated than it already was. But not telling had serious consequences for me.

Bottom line: There was no easy way out. The easy way was what Jackson had tried to take. What had landed us both in the hot seat in the first place.

Slowly, feeling as if I were literally dragging my feet, I made my way back to my locker. I stowed my gear, then paused in front of the row of colorful aprons. What on earth would be a good choice? Was there a color that said, *Help me! I don't know what to do!*

Maybe I should put on two, I thought. Blue for serenity—the strength to remain calm. Red for optimism—the ability to pray that things might still turn out all right.

"Oh, there you are, Grace," I suddenly heard Ms. Newberry's voice. It was hard, but I managed not to jump.

"Thank you so much for coming in. You made good time. Before you go out onto the floor, could you come into my office for a moment?"

She made a gesture, asking me to go on in ahead of her. I walked toward the office, doing my best not to wring my hands. My fingers felt like ice.

I swear the dozen or so steps from my locker to Ms. Newberry's office were the longest of my entire life. But by the time I made it there and heard the quiet click of the door as she closed it behind us, I knew what I had to do.

"Sit down, Grace," Ms. Newberry said. I couldn't detect any anger in her voice. And I was listening for it pretty darn hard.

"Ms. Newberry, there's something I have to tell you," I burst out. "And, if it's all the same to you, I think I would like to do it standing up."

Ms. Newberry walked around me till she faced me across her desk. She stayed standing, too.

"All right."

I'm pretty sure I did wring my hands then. But as I had lost all feeling in them by that point, it was hard to be sure.

"Something happened," I said. "The night I helped you cash out. I should have told you right away. I didn't and that was wrong. But I didn't do anything else, Ms. Newberry. You've got to believe that."

She was silent for a moment, gazing at me with thoughtful eyes.

"I do believe that, Grace," she said at last.

I felt my whole body flush. I could feel my knees begin to quiver.

"Please," Ms. Newberry said. "Go ahead and sit down. I won't feel comfortable sitting unless you do, too. We're going to be on our feet all day. I figure that means we should grab any chance to sit while we can."

"All day," I echoed as I sank slowly down into the chair that faced her desk. "You mean, I'm not fired?"

"No, you're not fired, Grace." Ms. Newberry folded her hands, resting them lightly on top of her desk.

"Jackson came to see me, first thing this morning. He was waiting out front when I came to open up the store. He told me everything that happened, including how upset you were. He also brought back that missing hundred dollars."

Maybe it was just the sudden relief, but I felt tears prick at the back of my eyes.

"I'm so glad he did that," I said. So glad he did what was right. Not that it let me entirely off the hook. "Ms. Newberry," I went on, "I know I probably should have come to you before now."

"There's no probably about it, Grace," she said. "Painful as it would have been for you both, you should have informed me at once.

"But I understand you have a loyalty to a friend, more than a friend, right? I may be almost old enough to be your mother, but I'm not completely out of touch with what it feels like to be young and in love."

"What's going to happen to Jackson?" I asked.

Ms. Newberry shook her head. "I think I'm going to let him tell you that, himself. What I can tell you is what's going to happen to you. I had planned to start training you to run the register. I'm going to delay that, now. This doesn't mean you won't ever be given that responsibility. It just means I intend to slow things down.

"I've been very impressed with you since I hired you, Grace," Ms. Newberry finished quietly. "I gave you a lot of trust. Some of that has been shaken by your recent actions."

"And now I need to earn it back," I said. "I will, I promise. I appreciate the fact that you're giving me a second chance. I know not everybody would."

"You're welcome," Ms. Newberry said. She stood up and so did I. "Now, I don't expect us to talk about this again, and I see no reason for you to mope about it. Let's just put it behind us and get back to business. I feel certain everything will work out fine."

She came around the desk and put an arm around my shoulders. "Lavender for creativity today, I think," she said. "It's time to start working on that Thanksgiving display window."

By the time I got off work it had stopped raining, but the day was still gray and cold. Working at the store had been pretty good. Following our discussion, Ms. Newberry and I had worked together on the Thanksgiving display window. She didn't make any other reference to the incident with the cash drawer. It wasn't quite as if it had never happened, but it did feel as if we were moving on.

A second chance. That's what she had given me.

I didn't feel like going home when my shift was over. It wasn't that I was feeling blue or bad. Not precisely. But I was definitely unsettled, still uncertain about what the future would hold for Jackson and me. I needed some time away from anything that reminded me of the last few weeks.

I knew just the place. The birdhouse at the science museum.

One of Greenwood's claims to fame is our science and natural history museum. Originally an old estate, one of the first big mansions in the area, it's located pretty much in the center of town—not all that far from Main Street and Alternate Realities.

My absolute favorite part of the museum has always been the birdhouse, which is essentially a big aviary. Only it's not just for the birds, it's for people as well. It has plants, trees, benches. It's sort of like a little minipark, under glass. It's a particularly great place to go when the weather gets nasty. No matter how grim it gets outside, inside the birdhouse it's always bright and warm. Matt and I had both loved to come here. It was my favorite thinking spot.

I checked in with my parents to let them know I would be another couple of hours, then made a purchase at Alternate Realities. A brand-new sketchbook and a new set of pencils. Then I headed on over to the birdhouse.

I strolled around a bit, finally settling on my favorite bench, just off the main path under a big oak tree. I tucked my legs up under me, set the sketchbook on my lap, and opened it up.

I gazed down at the fresh, clean page, letting the sounds of the birdhouse sort of flow around me, soothing and raucous all at once.

Clean page. Clean start, I thought.

I put my pencil on the paper and started to draw. After a few moments, an image began to appear. I was drawing one of the birds in the birdhouse. Not one of the brighter ones. The bird I sketched had a small head, a round smooth breast offset by a sweep of darker wings. I could even hear the call it made inside my head, soft cascading notes that always sounded sad.

Which is precisely how it got its name: mourning dove.

I did several different quick sketches of the bird in different positions, then turned to a new page as the images continued to flow.

I began to draw again. An entirely different image this time. Matt and Jackson together, like they'd been in that photo of the camping trip.

With just a few strokes, I had the outlines of the two of them together. I would fill in the details later.

What I wanted now was to be able to visualize what was in my mind. Around the two of them, as if in the background, I began to draw another bird. Bigger, with its wings upswept this time, as if about to take flight.

It was still a mourning dove. But it was also something more. It was a phoenix, rising from the ashes. A sign that both Jackson and Matt would make it through whatever challenges they faced. That we all would.

"Hey," I heard a sudden voice.

I jumped, and the pencil drew a jagged line across the paper. I looked up to see Jackson towering over me.

"Hey, yourself." There was an awkward pause. "How did you know where to find me?" I finally asked.

"I didn't," Jackson admitted with an attempt at a smile. "I, um, I come here to think sometimes. This seemed like a good day to do it, and here you are."

"I come here to think, too," I said. "And also to draw."

He stood for a moment, staring down at me, while I stared up at him. "You want to sit down?"

"Only if you want me to," Jackson said.

"It would be okay, I guess."

Jackson eased himself down onto the bench beside me. We listened to the birds for a moment.

"I saw Ms. Newberry today," I finally said. "She called me in, to sub for Shannon. She told me you'd come in and . . ." My voice trailed off.

"Confessed," Jackson said. "I think confessed is the word you're looking for. Yeah, I did. And I told the guys in the band, as well. I told them how I got the money for the extra fee and that I was going to give it back. . . . We had to drop out of the contest."

Jackson exhaled a long sigh, as if he had been holding his breath. "I thought telling Ms. Newberry was tough, and believe me, it was. But I think telling the guys I let them down was the hardest thing I've ever done."

"How did they handle it?" I asked.

"You know?" Jackson said, with just the slightest lift in his voice. "Better than I thought. Of course they weren't happy that I screwed up our chance, at first. But then they actually offered to go to AR with me when I went to talk to Ms. Newberry. You know, for moral support."

"What did you say to that?" I asked.

"Thanks, but no thanks," Jackson said. "I told them it was something I needed to do on my own."

He shifted position, so that he could look straight at me. "So anyway, I told Ms. Newberry everything I'd done. I said I would understand if she wanted to call the police. She said that wasn't necessary. I thought for sure she would fire me.

"Then she looked at me in that way she has—you know—the one she uses when she's trying to decide what color you should put on. She asked me if I was sorry for what I'd done. When I said yes, she asked what I thought my punishment should be."

"What did you say?"

"Well, of course I said I thought that she should fire me. But she said, 'What if I don't fire you?'

"I was so shocked I didn't know what to say. I said something like I shouldn't be allowed to work the cash register for a certain period of time. Like, maybe, the rest of my natural life.

"I said she should move me out of the music department into something I didn't like so well. She said yes to the first, but no to the second. She said . . ."

He broke off, as if trying to remember her exact words. "She said it was important for me to have a *stake* in my job. She told me that she's been wanting to do some community outreach stuff, music programs for underprivileged kids or something. She's putting me in charge of that. I mean, completely in charge.

"I have to come up with a list of program ideas, ways to implement them. That sort of stuff."

I could hear the excitement in his voice as he talked. It was a sound I hadn't heard in a very long time. Maybe not since Matt died. Not since he'd told me his parents were getting divorced, for sure.

Ms. Newberry, you are a genius, I thought. It seemed Philomena wasn't the only one who understood the need to open doors rather than slam them shut.

It was something I planned to keep in mind.

Jackson was quiet again, staring down at the bench. All of a sudden, it seemed to me that all the birds in the birdhouse fell silent.

"What about us, Grace?"

I felt my heart rate kick up a notch. What did I really want? Ms. Newberry had given Jackson a second chance. She'd given me one. Could I do the same?

Was being in a relationship with Jackson still what I wanted? Could I trust him?

I didn't answer.

Jackson broke the silence. "What I did was wrong. I was unfair to you but please don't give up on me, Grace. That's all I'm asking."

"I won't," I said. The words came out before I had a second to think. "I can't."

He dropped his head, like my words had just taken a huge weight off him. I scooted a little closer, and put my hand on his. He rested his chin on the top of my head. We sat, just like that, for I don't know how long. And all of a sudden, I realized the bird songs were back. Exuberant and joyful.

"I'm going to have to go," Jackson said after a while. "I told my mom I had to talk to her about something important."

"Good luck," I said, as we moved apart. We both stood up.

"Thanks, Grace," Jackson said. "I really mean that. I'll call you. Let you know how it goes."

"You'd better," I said. "So, I guess I'll see you around," Jackson said.

"Count on it," I replied.

I knew who I would see waiting for me as soon as I turned the corner to my street.

Philomena Cantos.

"Philomena!" I called out.

She smiled. Her cheeks were flushed pink by the cold air.

"Hi, Grace," she said. "How are you?"

"Jackson's going to be okay," I blurted out. "He told Ms. Newberry everything. She's being really great about it. Things are still tough with his family, but I think things will work out there, too. In the long run."

"And how about you?" Philomena asked. "Are you all right?"

"Yes, I am," I answered slowly. "In a whole lot of ways. Jackson and I are still good. But I think I also understand more about what you mean, now. The reason Jackson's going to get through all this is because *he* made the call. He decided what action he should take. Nobody else made it for him. Nobody else can, can they? Not even a person who *really* cares for him."

"That's right," Philomena said softly.

She turned to go.

"Wait a minute!" I cried. "You mean that's it? That's all? No more words of wisdom? No information about what we do now?"

"Grace," Philomena chided, but I could see just the hint of a twinkle in her eye. "That isn't the way this works. You ought to know that by now. We won't know where we're needed next until we do."

"*We,*" I said. "You mean I'll know, too? All on my own? I won't have to wait for you to tell me?"

"I didn't tell you to help Jackson, did I?"

"Well, no, you didn't," I acknowledged, as I realized it was true. "You just had an awful lot to say about how not to."

"I reserve the right to do that," Philomena said with a laugh.

She turned away again. "I have to go now."

"Philomena," I said. She paused but didn't look back. "When you're not with me, where do you go?

Do you, like, live somewhere? Do you have a house? A garage where you park your car?"

"I have what I need," Philomena said. "Do you really need to know more? I'll see you around, Grace. I'm looking forward to it. I hope you are, too."

She continued toward the sidewalk. I watched her, until she turned the corner and was gone.

Just before she disappeared, I heard a sound. Felt a funny puff of air in my face, as if something that had been held in check had been released. The day around me was completely still. Nothing else moved at all.

I know what that is, I thought. *I recognize that feeling, that sound.*

Somewhere, a new door had opened.